Weaving the Web of Days

a tale of the Scattered Worlds

by:
Don Sakers

WEAVING THE WEB OF DAYS
copyright © 2004, Don Sakers

Published by
Speed-of-C Productions
811 Camp Meade Rd
Linthicum, MD 21090

Weaving the Web of Days takes place in The Scattered Worlds
universe. In chronological sequence, it falls at 4.55. For more
information, visit the Scattered Worlds website at
www.scatteredworlds.com.

ISBN: 978-1-934754-23- 8

April 2020

DEDICATED TO

Sue Abromaitis
Datta. Dayadhvam. Damyatta.

Was life worth living then? and now
Is life worth sin?
Where are the imperial years? and how
Are you Faustine?

Your soul forgot her joys, forgot
Her times of teen;
Yea, this life likewise will you not
Forget, Faustine?

For in the time we know not of
Did fate begin
Weaving the web of days that wove
Your doom, Faustine.

– Swinburne

I.
"Lean back, and get some minutes' peace"
Xchurch, New Zealand, Terra
Solday, 28 February TE 219

Danger!

Danger?

Maj Thovold pulls herself upright in her sleep cocoon. A meter-high tetrahedron of brushed metal glides noiselessly over, hovering half a meter off the floor. The autoservant, triggered by her movement, awaits her command. She waves it away.

What awakened her? Fragments of a dream still cling: giant spiders the size of her fist, hitting the ground and bursting into thousands of pinhead-sized babies—a hint of danger, a taste of anxiety—but what the cause?

For half a second she ponders calling her Ministers, Defense and Security and all the others, demanding of them the source of her anxiety. Then sense returns. They would only say that the Empress is having bad dreams again, humor her, the old gal is getting no younger. Senile hallucinations.

So what if the Empress is getting old? Her hunches have saved them all, time and again.

And yet there *are* bad dreams, more now than when she was younger.

Maj rolls out of the warm cocoon and pulls a light robe about her. Seeing that she is on her way to the balcony, five autoservants race ahead, an assortment of geometric shapes ready to jump at an instant in case of an assassination attempt. Once Maj used Human bodyguards—she finds the cybs much more reliable. Besides, the Empress has ways to defend herself.

The night sky is alight with stars in their thousands. To her right Maj sees the outline of the dome that covers the city Xchurch, the few lights that still twinkle under the dome. New Zealand followed standing orders in preparing for the Empress' visit; her temporary palace is well outside the city dome. Maj doesn't like being within a city. She is always claustrophobic, knowing that a barrier stands between her and the open sky of a world. Never, in all her thousands of hours in Navy starships or within the curving walls of settlements orbiting free in space, has she felt the least bit cramped. Only on a world. Only under the domes.

She takes a deep, meditative breath and stretches, feeling for a moment like the reincarnation of one of her ancient Maori ancestors, come back through time and space to this valley once again. She smiles, and turns her eyes skyward.

Look at the stars, Ancestor, she says as if the flesh of her progenitor were before her. Alpha Centauri, Epsilon Indi, Epsilon and 40 Eridani...can you pick them out at the end of a pointing finger? They haven't moved since you sailed these trackless waters in your canoe. The centuries that separate you and I are nothing to the stars. Ah, but you have not seen the *worlds* of those stars, worlds that I have walked upon. Euphrates, Metikos, Flajol and Promethia—the massed cities and settlements of those planets, four billion souls owing allegiance to Terra and her Empire—and these are but the beginning.

Over twenty-five hundred inhabited worlds, Ancestor, and probably ten times as many settlements. Could I name them for you, even if I knew all their names? It would take far too long, and an Empress needs her sleep.

A sleepless night's worth of names, Maj thinks, hugging her robe about her. Hours and hours of planets all across the Galaxy, all members of the Terran Empire. And she, their Empress.

Nearly two trillion Human souls in the Galaxy: all served and protected, fed and kept happy, by the day after-day work of Maj Thovold and all her subordinates.

And not only this Galaxy alone. For our ships have reached further, and our explorers have stood on the shoals of other star-islands. You would be proud of us, my distant forbear who set out in a reed canoe to find a land you didn't know existed.

Maj squints—three corneal transplants make her eyes work. but nothing can ever make them see as they had when she was young, and she is too proud to use artificial aids—squints, and sees what she is looking for, two pale clouds of starstuff high in the heavens.

From nowhere, a shiver and a dream-memory come to her, and she stiffens. The Magellanic Clouds? Is *this* where the lies? Were those the Clouds in her dream, or just swirls in the turbulent atmosphere of almost any Terran world? And by what right does she place credence in the warning of what was, after all, only a dream?

"I am the Empress," she whispers, half to herself and half to her ancestor. "'I do as I please."

Danger.

Maj frowns. Danger means change. And change all too likely means entropy. With war conquered and most forms of Human suffering under control, entropy is the last thing she wants loosed upon the Empire (and upon Humanity, for aren't the two synonymous?) Maj Thovold bears entropy an antagonism almost personal. Entropy is the greatest enemy of this Admiral-turned-Empress.

She holds out her wrinkled hands, lets a rueful smile cross her lips. Entropy is winning the battle. Joints creak a little, these days, and too much dampness starts up unpleasant reverberations of pain in her bones. It is long past time that she should have something done, if she doesn't want entropy to claim another victory. With a word, the best gerontologists in the Galaxy are at her service.

Why bother? she fancies her Ancestor asking. She turns back to the city and the stars.

For them, Ancestor. For two trillion people who have yet to produce one among their number who could manage this Empire half as well as I. Because if I take my peace, the next day the chiefs of half a dozen Idara will be swarming over the Palace clawing one another for my position. And not one of them is strong enough to hold it, if she *did* manage to reach the Throne.

The balcony railing is comfortingly solid beneath hands that quiver a bit. We had the rule of the Imperial Council, nearly two centuries of constitutional oligarchy before I came along and took over. And it took twenty years to clean up the mess made by too many cooks. You didn't see it as I did, Ancestor. Some worlds where excess food went to waste as reaction mass, and others only a kiloparsec away where people starved, children with distended bellies and empty eyes, just because they were across a boundary of Idara control. Can I let that happen again, no matter what it costs me?

She lets a sigh join the night breeze. If danger were coming, from the Magellanic Clouds or wherever else, she had to be prepared to meet it. To deal with the changes it brought. I am not dead, can not accept death—and a living being must respond to change.

At least it will—she can hope—break the daily tedium of the Imperial Court, the never-ending succession of crises which surround her.

The Magellanic Clouds. Hmm....

She limps back to bed, imagining relief in the way the guardian autoservants scurry back to their cubbyholes.

There are no more dreams that night.

II.
"A star upon your birthday burned"
Tarantula Nebula, Large Magellanic Cloud
Solday, 28 February TE 219

"Of course I'm a rebel." Paula Adelhardt lifts a white, vaguely-spongy morsel to her mouth and sniffs. The same syntho-stuff as yesterday, with a flavor slightly reminiscent of fish and a texture like foam rubber. She gulps it down, makes a face, and takes a quick drink of water. With luck, the water in her bottle will last the meal. "I spent my formative years on Leikeis, remember, hotbed of the Engelbach Rebellion."

"The Engelbachs never had a great following—and you can hardly call a tenday strike a rebellion." For once Paula envies her companion, Drav Lokys. Cyborgs never eat. It might be worth the transformation, to be spared this meal.

"Nevertheless," she continues, "When I came up the air was full of the Engelbachs and it was considered great fun to buck Authority. All the kids did it. Look at the holodramas of twenty years ago—we were raised on a steady diet of rebel, rebel, rebel."

She brushes back her long ebony hair. "Of course, now we're grown up and we are Authority. And now we have the chance we wanted all along, to change the system."

Drav produces a laugh. "How much change do you think you'll actually accomplish?"

She pushes her plate away into the grip of a hovering autoservant. "Probably only one in a thousand of us will ever amount to anything. I intend to be that one. Look at it logically—I'm in the best position to work massive change. Fifty kiloparsecs from home, out of contact with the Empire except for one mail ship every tenday; almost total command of a place that very obviously needs reforming…it would be harder to avoid accomplishing something."

Drav laughs again, moves on his antigrav. Then movement and sound stop. One of his cameras drifts away from Paula's face.

"What is it?"

Drav holds up one waldo, claw splayed. "Just a second." He floats poised almost like a dog straining after a distantly-heard twilight bark. Then both his cameras focus on her. "Get your vacuum suit on and follow me. We have trouble."

"What?" It still takes a conscious effort to reach for her vacuum suit, to pull the coarse fabric tight over her body. She'd been through tendays of drills before she even arrived, and they continued during the six tendays she's been here—but one became lazy, living in the Headquarters pressure-volume.

It is nearly ninety seconds before she closes the last seal and is ready to move against spring resistance of heavily-woven fibers. A little puter display within her helmet signals that her suit is properly sealed.

By this time Drav is halfway down the main corridor towards the docking bays. Paula trots to catch up with him. "What's happening?"

"Omega Sohrab has flared up." Strange to hear Drav's voice dimly carried through the permaplastic of her helmet as well as sharply on the comm. "It's been moving through the Web toward an inhabited volume for years now; the flare shell will reach those regions much sooner. We have to evacuate them."

They reach the docking bay, a cavernous space outlined with bright red guide lights. Four Imperial Navy Class G Troop Carriers and two Class N Gunboats are in dock. Paula unsnaps her datapad from her belt and punches an inquiry, smiles at what the tiny screen shows. The remaining two ships of her small fleet are on detached duty around the Nebula; they are answering the summons to Omega Sohrab and will arrive quickly, perhaps even before the main fleet.

She dashes aboard the Headquarters gunboat, Quick Punch, with barely time to greet the Captain, then straps into an acceleration couch on the bridge. She grins. The eight weeks she's been in command of Tarantula Facility have all been like this, crisis after crisis. Through it all, she is learning more and more about the job that her father left in such a muddle. Soon, now, she should be able to start working on the real task, the reforms so desperately needed.

The ship launches.

The sky is bleached muslin in all directions, tinted here and there with rainbow streaks and jots and textured eddies that veil stars-to-be. Seen from within, the Tarantula Nebula is most impressive. Yet something else draws her eye and her mind. This chalk-picture beauty is everywhere overlaid with a tar-splatter of filament, reticule, and globule: the Web.

Debates still rage in the Empire, a generation after the Web's creation, about its nature. That it is organic cannot be denied—the genetic labs of Hlekkar and other settlements did their jobs well. Formed of complex molecules of nebular hydrogen, oxygen, nitrogen, and carbon—plus a smattering of other elements—the Web is a strong, flexible network of endless chains of self-replicating molecules that absorb starlight and use its energy to feed continuing growth.

The chemical nature of the Web is not at issue—detailed records and analyses are in the Imperial Library. But is the Web alive? It grows. It produces mutated sections beyond the predictions of its creators. It concentrates thinly scattered spaceborne molecules and produces atmospheres, proteins and amino acids, even a leavening of trace elements that serve to keep Human beings alive. Through a volume measuring over five hundred cubic parsecs and still growing, the Web stitches together a fragile set of environments that just barely keeps its inhabitants from death.

In all this immense volume, the Web takes on many forms. Tendrils stretch across lightyears superconducting flashes of current; habitable regions hang suspended in the biospheres of newborn stars, with pockets of oxy-nitrogen and oxy-helium and water; apparently free-floating globules connect with the body of the Web by diamond threads, responding to light, heat, gravity, magnetism like colossal, fragile sensory organs—and somewhere in the unexplored cubic parsecs of the Web are rumored huge lumps of tissue that resemble neural or circuit patterns, great brains the size of continents, dreaming their own visions incomprehensible to the maggots that crawl among their far-flung strands....

Quick Punch dips into tachyon phase and back out, lightyears in a few breaths. Omega Sohrab is a brilliant disk on the viewscreens, a disk with black cobwebs silhouetted against it and stretching behind it. All around the star is the chromatic beauty of gas-shells interacting with nebula dust and the fabric of the Web itself.

"Wolf-Rayet stars are like that," Drav tells her. "Too active for their own good—throwing off shells of atmosphere the way other stars throw off flares."

Paula shields her eyes and squints at the Web. "People should have known better than to settle this near to such an unstable star."

"They didn't have much of a choice. Omega Sohrab isn't motionless, you know. Most of the stars in this Nebula have irregular proper motions. Too much gravitational disturbance. They were safely beyond any shell-danger when they settled years ago. Sixty kilometers per second is pretty fast, when it's a star flying at your habitat and getting closer each day."

"We should have done something sooner." The inhabitants of the Web have no starships—which is the whole point of locating them in a dense nebula in the Greater Magellanic Cloud. No ships, terrific gravitational strain that would wreck any but the most durable antigravs, and throughout the whole galaxy a dearth of the vital and delicate tachyon vesicles so necessary to build antigravs and tachyon converters. After all, the Empire has a vested interest in seeing that none of the prisoners sent to the Web ever escaped. Still, leaving the people without ships made it even more necessary that the Empire be ready to succor them in situations like this one.

"If the star hadn't burped so far ahead of schedule," Drav says, his mechanical voice unemotional, "they would have been all right. As it is, we're here to rescue them now, so what does it matter?"

As they speak, the rest of the fleet appears. All the Imperial ships in the Greater Magellanic Cloud are gathered here in this hollow of the Web.

The Captain leans forward in his command chair. "Jambo. What's that?" He touches his lapboard; one viewscreen zooms onto a section of the Web less than a million kilometers away, hours from the expanding gas shell. "That's in our records as the primary area of settlement here."

"What's going on?" Drav reaches out a waldo and plugs a contact into control panel before him; Paula imagines he's receiving visual impressions directly from ship's instruments.

The viewscreen image jiggles and fuzzes, then ship's comp firms it up. The magnification tightens, and Paula starts to get an idea of what she is seeing.

Diminutive Human figures in vacuum suits are tethered to the fibers of the Web, surrounding a large nodule of Web-stuff. They look like insects swarming on a tree, carpenter ants entering their burrows as they squeeze one-by-one into a hole in the nodule. At some signal, a few of the Humans stop the flow and seal the open hole. The remaining crowd draws back and the nodule stirs, tears itself free from the Web, and spreads a gigantic reflective sail that balloons out under light pressure. The irregularly-shaped nodule moves against the brightness of Omega Sohrab, while those left behind move on across the Web to another waiting nodule.

The view shifts; Drav points with a waldo. "Focus on that."

Another such nodule, this one with a fully-extended sail, much closer to the gas shell. The view hunts, and Paula sees yet another nodule, and another still further away, and….

"Ship says they're curving around the star just outside the gas shell. The outer surface of the nodules is ablative. If we could see beyond the star, I'll bet we'd see more of those hulks paraboling around to the other edge of the Web."

"We have just learned of the danger, and all this time they've been saving themselves." The orbits of those nodules have to be tendays long…Paula's mind boggles at the concerted effort necessary to build and launch rescue vessels with no raw materials but the Web.

View returns to the original site. There are only a hundred or so people in evidence; they are busily clambering about a much smaller nodule.

Drav emits a sound of pity. "That final vessel isn't going to succeed. They miscalculated the star's eruptive period just as we did. The last three launched are going to be hit by the plasma shell."

"For stars' sakes, go rescue them. Put one troop carrier on each of those three nodules...tow them to a safe place where they can be released. "

Drav gives orders. "What about the people at the launch site?"

"We'll pick them up ourselves." Paula touches her own controls, recessed in the arm of her couch; the view zooms even tighter, reaching the extreme limit of magnification. One figure, in a bright red vacuum suit, is apparently in charge; she cannot distinguish a face, but every gesture carries command.

"That must be their leader. I want to talk with her." As the new Administrator of the Tarantula Facility, she needs to learn more about the lives and living conditions of the prisoners.. If she is going to do any good in the long run, she needs to know what she fights against. Besides, a man who could lead a fantastic operation like this one, would be a powerful ally among the prisoners.

Antigravs surge, and Quick Punch moves toward the launch site as yet another part of the Web is consumed by Omega Sohrab's fiery breath.

III.
"The shapely silver shoulder stoops"
Tarantula Nebula, Large Magellanic Cloud
Solday, 28 February TE 219

Tsung-Dao Wu peels off his bright red vacuum suit as he enters his ship through the starboard airlock, stuffs it into a too-small locker and slams the door. Close. Entirely too close.

The pilot, a long-time veteran of Tarantula who was once an Imperial Navy Captain, awaits him just inside the lock. She is barely waist-high, her white hair bound in a ponytail that clings to her right shoulder. Tsung-Dao grasps her hand warmly. "Smooth maneuvering, Thena. Thanks. The authorities didn't even realize that your ship was in orbit."

Pilot nibbles at a fingernail. "They're stupid. They expect no ships, so they look not for ships. Never would I have fooled them, had they bothered to scan."

Stupid? Tsung-Dao, fresh from three hours with the new Administrator, shakes his head. No, Paula Adelhardt is not stupid. Just...untried. "Just as well they didn't." The ship is a patched-together model based on the hull of an old cargo-transport—large as it is, a handful of people can crew it. They are all in the control room as Tsung-Dao follows Pilot in. Ostensibly, the crew are at their workstations; from sidewise looks and whispered comments, Tsung-Dao knows that they are all waiting for him to say something.

On the main viewscreen, Omega Sohrab blazes behind a tracery of Web. Tsung-Dao takes his seat, front and center, and spins to face his people.

"All right, that was a near thing. If the Imperials had come two hours earlier, they'd have seen you towing Web modules and our secrecy would be blown. As it is, every one of you acted correctly in the emergency, and I want to commend you on that. I spent quite some time with the new Imperial Administrator and I'm all but certain she doesn't know about our fleet." He remembers Paula's manner, her intensity as she sat across a dinner in High Imperial style. Is she playing with him? No—the woman wears her insides on her skin, unless Tsung-Dao is drastically mistaken. She doesn't know.

Pilot starts on another fingernail. "Where go we now? Suppose you'll be making a report to Headquarters?"

Tsung-Dao understands the note of hesitancy in Pilot's question. Nobody wants to go to Headquarters, least of all those who have been there before. The way is long and treacherous, a winding path through the Web with no landmarks other than the navicomp's programming. And then there is Headquarters itself....

"Of course I have to report. If the new Administrator's going to be nosing around a lot, we may have to curtail some of our starship flights." And that would hurt. For the first time in decades the precarious settlements of the Web are trading, thanks to ships like this one and the rest of the fleet. He required circumspection, only scheduling the most necessary flights—any curtailment in schedules mean that some community somewhere will be on short rations. Food, oxy-nitrogen, metals, the fibers so desperately needed to repair vacuum suits, water...there would be hard times.

He shrugs. The cutting of cargo schedules is a matter to take up with Headquarters. Worrying about it now does not good. "I know nobody likes the idea, but we have to go. Might as well get it over with."

Travel through the Web is never easy. In Zain, the long-settled volume Tsung-Dao originally called home, there is a mass driver and long-distance rapidtrans network. But building such amenities takes forever, dependent on the ever-scanty supply of metals, metals forged from lighter elements in reactors far hotter than the birthing stars of the Nebula.

There is no good way to get from place to place in the Web. The distances are too far, the settlements too separated. The closest they came to a good transportation system was starships. Starships in the shadowy existence of tachyon phase were hardly bothered by the physical obstacles presented by Webstrands. Naturally, each time a ship stepped over a strand in tachyon phase, it meant one more strain on delicate antigravs and tachyon converters. In the twenty years

Tarantula ships had been running regularly, already nearly a tenth of the original vessels had needed replacement antigravs.

Slowly, then, carefully the ship moves forward, zapping in and out of tachyon phase for microseconds as dictated by the navicomp. Finally the last tachyon conversion carries them into a large hollow pocket of Web-stuff, a cavity the size of a large planetoid, lit only by the ship's running lights. Directly before them, large mass of Web glints underneath like strong metal. They have reached Headquarters.

As the ship makes final approach, Tsung-Dao makes his way to the airlock and pulls on his vacuum suit. Cycling the lock, he dives from the ship.

Outside the ship's grav-field, Tsung-Dao casually pulls himself hand-over-hand across a hundred or so meters to the nearest airlock into the Headquarters compound. Like other convicts, Tsung-Dao was dumped in the Web by an Imperial ship with nothing but his vacuum suit and a tenday's rations. He knows the tug of vacuum on skin, the scramble across sticky Web-strands for a bit of food or a recharge dose of oxy-nitrogen; he knows the struggle to find a minuscule pocket that would support life for a while, hurried minutes of closeness beneath the light of strange suns before the air ran out and it was time to run again.

Of all Tarantulans, Tsung-Dao feels most equipped to appreciate the glories of Headquarters. Once scion of one of the highest-ranking Idara of all Earth, cast down to eke out an existence more by force of will than anything else, here in the Web he has built a place where people can live, can manage to think about things beyond mere survival. He has known the extremes and all between them; and he knows that Headquarters is luxury.

When the last of three airlock doors opens before him, They are waiting. She stands straight and thin in artificial one-third grav, her light hair falling about her shoulders. A clinging black gown traced with whirlpools of darker black barely conceals her withered yet still impressive figure. He sits, as He usually does—an active life of over a century has left muscles and nerves unwilling to fight even a lower grav than standard.

His hands are still strong, though, nearly waldo-strong on the controls of his chair. With eyes like dark holes in the substance of the Nebula, They gaze at Tsung-Dao, and he feels a touch like an icy dagger traced between his shoulderblades.

Every once in a while, when he's far away from Them, Tsung-Dao feels ridiculous thinking in capital letters and honorifics—but there is no other way for an ordinary mortal to think about Them. Only a cretin—or a great fool—could fail to be impressed by Brin Lütken and Catherine Leonov, late Masayyid of the Terran Empire. An entire generation had grown up with Sayyid Brin and Sayyid Catherine as surrogate mother and father. Protectors of the poor and helpless, dispensers of justice, through Their three decades on the Imperial Council, They ruled the Empire like no one ever before.

Tsung-Dao himself is a child of that rule. Masayyid Brin and Catherine are figures out of his childhood myths, the good folk who stood in the way of every demon, the legitimate darlings of the Council and the Galaxy, the role model of every Idara child possibly destined for government.

"Why are you here?" Sayyid Catherine's voice is raspy, yet still Tsung-Dao hears, as if dopplered through time, the reflection of power that once shook a Galaxy. Her eyes, darker and colder than intergalactic gulfs, fasten on him and suck the heat from his soul.

"The new Imperial Liaison brought her fleet to Omega Sohrab. She didn't see any of our ships, and in a dinner afterward I got the impression that she doesn't have any suspicions."

Sayyid Brin rolls his eyes. "Oh, that. It was predicted that she would show up. I told you there was no need to send ships for that rescue."

"It was close. People might have died if our ships hadn't been there. We barely had enough pods to carry them all." Time to stick his neck out. "As a matter of fact, I wish you'd given me a few of the transports. We wouldn't have had to worry about the pods."

Catherine puts a hand on her husband's shoulder, as if to restrain him from rising up to tear out Tsung-Dao's throat. "And where would we be, when the Imperials showed up and found no people there? There would be an investigation, and in it they might locate our fleet."

Tsung-Dao shakes his head. His vacuum suit is uncomfortably hot, but he doesn't want to take it off; he has no desire to stay longer than necessary. "Our fleet is too well hidden. The Empire isn't going to discover that we're planning a revolution."

"They will if you do not keep a tighter rein on your tongue," Sayyid Brin counters.

"I've said nothing improper."

Sayyid Catherine looks into the middle distance. "'Revolution.' Dalinka, you have such a melodramatic way. I assure you, if Maj Thovold thought we were planning a revolution, she would sleep soundly in that absurd cocoon of hers." She scratches at an invisible fleck on the permaplastic of Brin's chair-back. "Tell the Empress that we are coming in force to kill her, then she will take you seriously."

"Whatever you like. We needn't fret about Maj learning our secrets through the new Liaison."

Brin smiles. "As if we ever did."

"You know her?"

"Paula Adelhardt is espoused to a son of ours, name of Rand."

"Grandson, dear."

"Whichever. She is a worthless child only a little more energetic than her parent. Jeremy gave us no difficulty…I doubt his daughter is perceptive enough to divine our dreadful secrets."

Sayyid Catherine leans forward. "All the same, we want you to keep your eyes on Paula Adelhardt. She is one of those reform-minded liberals, and the databanks have it that she is committed to reforming this facility. Shutting it down, ultimately. That would be unfortunate for her. We need an extragalactic base." Catherine shows her teeth. "Ironic, nyet?

No one thinks of looking among criminals and traitors, for the two people who are proclaimed the Empire's worst enemies."

"The irony escapes me. I'd like permission to start the process of moving Omega Sohrab settlements to a safer location. In twenty years we can build a bank of gas-lasers to launch relativistic escape pods." Tsung-Dao led his own people to construct such a system many years ago. Now six Web-pods fly at nearly lightspeed toward distant portions of the Greater Magellanic Cloud, toward promise of habitable planets.

"Where do you expect to get the metals and other building materials?"

"I also want to construct some new reactors in the region."

Catherine sighs. "This becomes steadily more complicated. Constructing a reactor ties up ships and materials for years. Our plans are coming to a head, Tsung-Dao. We have neither ships nor materials to spare."

"I won't be put off like a spoiled child. Those people are in danger as long as they remain in the biosphere of a Wolf-Rayet star."

She puts on a suffering look. "Let the people remain until there is another dangerous flare. At that time, if it occurs, I give you my word that I will release enough troop transports to take them to a safe area of the Web. Does this satisfy you?"

Tsung-Dao lets his own lips curl in a smile. There is a feeling of exhilaration in playing well a game with the masters. "I am satisfied."

"Good. Now run along. I imagine Sayyid Paula will contact you again in the near future. According to Rand, she is quite vulnerable to a pretty face. And she is far from home." She squints. "You look a little like Rand, come to think of it. Keep your senses sharp, and tell us whatever you think is useful."

Sayyid Brin raises a hand in simultaneous benediction and dismissal. "And for stars' sakes try to talk her out of attempting to close down this facility. Tell her all about your own liberal days and how being shipped to the Imperial prison spaces taught you the error of your ways. With luck she will pity you, and be convinced." Both Brin and Catherine laugh, and Tsung-Dao turns back to the airlock.

Let them laugh, he thinks as vacuum embraces him. They're old and settled in their own patterns—and who can blame them? But he still feels the pull of his youthful idealism. Somewhere, he knows, there is a better world. And Tsung-Dao Wu can still have some part in bringing it to be.

IV.
"And all were smooth to spin"
Tarantula Nebula, Large Magellanic Cloud
Solday, 28 February TE 219

The place to which Catherine repairs has no name. It needs none—it is the only place of its kind in the universe, and she and Brin the only people who know of its existence. Any name would be superfluous.

In that place, she strips off her gown, exposing age-darkened skin crossed by the lighter lines of incisions. Her skin is pocked with puckered depressions, input sockets for her various implants. Little of Catherine Leonov's insides are as they were in her prime—medical and cybernetic technology worked their way upon her long ago. Without it, she would be long since dead.

Settling into a couch, she plugs a heavily-shielded cable into her left side, closes her eyes.

Alive! Once more, Catherine is alive in a way no lesser creature could ever imagine.

Images take form around her like nightdreams. Darkness, lit by stars and pale wisps of gas. This is how it has to be—her mind turns the Web's sensory impressions into something she can visualize, concrete images that a merely-human brain can understand.

I am Catherine Leonov…I am the Web. Am I not awesome?

A smile curls on her dry lips. The Empire does not know everything, nor do the pathetic convicts that Tsung-Dao works himself into a tizzy over. She, Catherine, knows what they can not: that the Web is riddled with her own ultrawave transmitters, compact half-organic sets beaming back to this place the impressions and currents that dance along the Web's tangled strands. She knows, as they can not, that from this couch she can become the Web, feel as it feels and make it move as she wills. From here, the rudimentary life functions of the Web are Catherine's to command, to shape at her will.

Catherine Leonov surveys her domain and loses herself in its wideness.

There is the Web itself. She feels each little tension in its structures, tensions caused by the movement of stars and planets, by the eddying of gases of the Tarantula Nebula, even by the activities of Humans. She narrows her perception around the region of Omega Sohrab, feels the delightful pain of an open gash as Webstuff vaporizes in expanding shells of plasma.

Outward from the Web and the Nebula she turns her attention, outward to light waves that have spent millennia on their journeys. Outward to the Greater Magellanic Cloud, in which the Web sits like a cancer in a living body.

Again Catherine's lips curl. Life, with all its tenacity, has infested the Web and the Nebula—but the Cloud itself is still untouched. Oh, not in the distant past. Evidence remains of at least three major galactic civilizations in both Magellanic Clouds. The last of these civilizations used up all the Cloud's tachyon vesicles half a billion years ago, and without vesicles there could be no stardrive, no ultrawave communication, no defense screens, no antigravity.

Perhaps remnants of those civilizations still huddle on planets in the Clouds. Perhaps their ships navigate interstellar space at lightspeed or below. If so, only by accident would they ever come to the attention of Humanity. Too much to get done, no one could spare time for a search of all the waste spaces of a galaxy, even one as small as this.

That suits Catherine. In an empty galaxy, no one can argue with her right to command. In an empty galaxy, no one can stop her.

All is well with the Web. Feeling regret, she removes the plug from her side and opens her eyes. Brin waits by the entrance, looking like a lost child in search of its crechenanny.

"How goes the Web?" he asks.

"Well." There is no other answer. She rises, pulls her overgown about her, and goes to him. She rests casually on the arm of his chair, feeling the chair shift to keep its balance.

"We handled Tsung-Dao well, don't you think? "

To herself, Catherine tsks. No need for Brin to make such a statement, no need for him to seek encouragement and support from her. For years she has watched her husband's slow design, has watched him measure by measure lose his self-confidence and drive. She has seen the encroaching weakness, and she can do nothing about it but feel a quiet melancholy.

"Yes," she answers, trying to keep a patronizing tone out of her voice. "We did well." Brin is still more than a match for any normal opponent...and yet she has begun to doubt if he could survive against their ultimate enemy, that renegade Navy commander who now calls herself Empress.

Brin was always weak. He stood against Maj Thovold longer than she did, long after their power all but faded away in the Imperial Council. She remembers one particular day, rather late in the whole conflict, when then-Admiral Thovold petitioned the Council for an increase in the Navy's budget. Seeing all the sycophants rush to agree, Catherine turned away and felt sick. It was Brin who faced their enemy.

"I do not think," he said sweetly, "That we need worry about increasing funding to the Navy. Much as we appreciate your function as a police force, Admiral Thovold, we cannot take the vast sums you require from capital development, just to increase your efficiency by a marginal few tenths of a percent."

"But Terrad says...."

Brin let Condescending Smile Number Three settle onto his features. "My dear Admiral, the Terran Defense Network has not been used since the end of the Formation Wars. I assure you, Earth is in no danger. I think we can all afford to disregard what Terrad says regarding an increase in its own budget."

Brin carried the day, then. A year later, his victory turned to ashes, for Maj Thovold was Empress, warships hovered above every major world in the Empire, and not even Brin's most persuasive smile influenced the suddenly-insane voters at home to grant him and his wife another term on the Council.

For that vanished power, for her husband's decline, for the years they spent as exiles—and for much, much more—this time Catherine intends to win.

Even the likes of Maj Thovold cannot defeat a weapon as powerful as the Web.

Especially when that weapon is directed by a singular, superior mind...like that of Catherine Leonov.

V.
"Where are the imperial years?"
New York, Terra
Friday, 26 March TE 219

Ever since her trip to New Zealand, Maj has imagined that the Maori ancestor she conjured out of a sleepless night is still with her, watching over her as she runs the Empire. It is an irrational delusion, one she fights whenever it occurs—yet at the oddest times she looks up from her compterm, and feels ghostly eyes upon her.

The mind is slipping. Soon she will have to call the gerontologists…if she wants to.

Thirty-two years I've given them, she tells her Ancestor. Thirty-two years that have worn me like three hundred. Flesh can be regenerated, transplanted, cloned, and cleaned until it is baby-fresh. Not so the human will.

I don't want to be Empress any more!

She shakes her head. Next she'll be talking aloud with her apparitions. She picks up a container of tiny green pills from the corner of her desk, puts it down again. For three decades those pills have sat on the desktop; she has yet to take one. Happy-drugs are not for the head of the Empire. Without her inhibitions, she might make mistakes. The pills are there only to remind her of her duty.

Duty, crap. You know you love it, Maj. Admit it—you like the ego boost of being the sole force standing between two trillion people and total chaos.

I have never tried to deny that.

Maj slides her chair back and allows it to stroke her lightly. Eyes closed, she places a hand on a scan-plate. At a bell-tone she open her eyes, allowing a low-power laser to scan her retinas. There is a tingle at her fingertip as the scan-plate's nanoprobes test her blood.

No mere palm- and retinal-prints for this machine: it is not satisfied until genotype, electroencephalogram, and RNA memory-track verification proves that she is indeed Maj Thovold.

From ultra-secure bunkers deep in the planet's crust, the Terrad system flashes its ready signal on Maj's datascreen.

Since her days as Supreme Admiral, when she first convinced the Secretary-General of the Empire to give her access to Terrad, the Terran Defense System had been her most trusted confidant. Terrad's memory banks are safe beyond the meaning of the word; the system consists of three interlocked Valkyrie computers, any one of which can pass any test ever designed for sapience.

"This is Maj Thovold. I have problems."

•Tell me.•

Maj ponders. Every morning psych-techs spend half an hour with her, imprinting upon her brain all the significant events of the last twenty-four hours; the information is there, but it takes a definite effort to access it. An effort that grows more difficult with each passing day.

"The Thieves' School has started issuing overtly political statements. Before this, they've been decidedly apolitical."

•They denounced the Imperial Council for attempting to veto your request for increased funding to new colonies. There is no need for concern...they seem to be on your side.•

"The Terrorist Guild shows an increase in activity of 15% over last year. Significant?"

•The significance is not readily apparent. We can conjecture, but there is not enough information for a meaningful prediction.•

"The Navy is catching more smugglers."

•No increase in Navy efficiency in reported. We surmise that smugglers are becoming clumsier.•

"That's a bad sign." Maj isn't sure where all these data are leading; she is simply trying to pick out items from this morning's report that jar. Much of her work is instinct, intuition. "The black market price of tachyon vesicles has jumped another three percentage points. That's a total increase of —"

•—Sixty-eight percent in the last year, up ninety-eight percent from ten years ago. We have been paying special attention to this trend. Possible explanations include difficulties in delivery due to the decrease in successful smuggling, and the remaining glut on the legal market from the large finds in Neordan Province three years ago.•

"Or someone's building a secret fleet. Something's making illegal vesicles pretty scarce."

Terrad pauses. The most irritating thing about sapient computers was how they would pause now and again for dramatic effect, just when one most wanted to take advantage of their speed. •Our intelligence reports indicate that the Empire is calm all over. We find no trace of incipient rebellion.•

How different from thirty years ago. At the start of her reign, Terrad found rebellion plots at a rate of six per hour. The rate has been dropping for years; she regularly went a hundred days or so between plots. And always the plots are stopped early, always they are of no consequence.

Until now?

"Someone's covered their tracks well, if they've been able to fool your intelligence pickups."

•It's a big Galaxy, Maj. Even we can't watch everything. We have developed a list of ten exponent five places where a rebellion could be headquartered, totally invisible to our intelligence. Chances approach certainty that there are at least another ten exponent three places we haven't yet projected.•

"And we can't reason or intuit our way through the problem. We have to wait until this rebellion shows itself."

•If your intuition is correct, and there is a rebellion at all.•

"Demn, I am so sick of this." She taps her fingers absently over the keys of her terminal; the screen scolds her until she stops. "Terrad—suppose I retire?"

•Abdicate.•

"I'm the first Empress, I can set whatever terminology I wish."

•We would not advise it.•

"Why not? 'Retire' is a perfectly good word."

•We do not advise that you retire.• Terrad has a tolerable sense of humor; Maj reflects that her joke was feeble. •You have not found a successor able to govern in your inimitable fashion.•

She is about to protest that her job isn't that hard—but she and Terrad both know the truth. Who else could tell House Chen, as she did today, to surrender half their carefully stockpiled protein reserves from Vetret to feed Patala? And without compensation? Each day is filled with similar tasks like that, not to mention the harder jobs she undertakes because she stands above Idara disputes and sees the long-range goals of the Empire.

Who would go through the grueling memory-implant sessions every morning, knowing that the process ages her a tenday? Having sat through those sessions, who would make proper use of the data thus implanted?

Who else could make the Navy listen to her?

"Suppose I don't worry about a successor? Suppose I just quit and go off to live on one of the new colonies under an assumed name?"

•If we thought that was a realistic alternative, we would prepare a contingency plan to deal with it. Knowing you as we do, your Majesty, we can spare our effort.•

Condemn it, Terrad is right. Weary as she is, sick of handling all their petty quarrels and childish bickering…she still cannot walk away from the job without leaving it in competent hands.

"Inform me when you get a lead on the identity of this rebellion," she says, preparing to switch off the Terrad link.

•It is possible that you will know before we do, Maj. The architects of this current rebellion may try to emulate their most successful precursors by attempting to lure you into a trap.•

"Traps don't scare me. I've outthought all of them so far."

•The converse need be true only once,• Terrad reminds her, then switches off of its own accord.

Maj stares at the blank screen for long seconds. Yes, she's beaten every trap so far, beaten them long before they were sprung. But twice now she's noticed signs of her mental abilities failing. Is she able to outwit the next trapper?

Especially—she thinks of the Magellanic Clouds floating serenely above Christchurch—especially if the next trapper is who she half-expects. By all accounts, if there is a rebellion in the works, it is being expertly run by someone extraordinarily subtle and very, very careful.

In thirty-two years, there is still one quarrel left unsettled — and all gods know They are subtle and careful. Both of Them....

She shrugs and turns back to her work.

VI.
"A shadow of laughter like a sigh"
Fringes of the Milky Way Galaxy
Tuesday, 3 April TE 219

Paula is glad to be back in touch with civilization. The thing she hates most about the Greater Cloud, is that the Empire cannot afford to string the vast number of ultrawave relays needed to put Tarantula in instant contact. In an age in which every inhabited planet can communicate with every other in instants, being out of touch is a nearly unendurable hardship.

As her shuttle comes within ultrawave range of the Milky Way, Paula finds her datascreen suddenly alight with the prerecorded messages of the last tenday. She skims through them quickly: some Idara business, a few personal letters, little else.

She handles the Idara business simply by referring it to her father. One reason the Adelhardts were chosen to oversee the Tarantula project, she is sure, is the Idara's unique policy of gesammenverhandlung, which holds all Adelhardt-administered properties in common. For convenience, one person in each generation is designated as Heir. Derian Sayyid Cepeda, Duke of Geled, is one who needs to be on the spot to manage his Province; although Paula succeeded her father as Administrator of the Adelhardt factories on and near Leikeis, she is free to go off to the Greater Cloud in the secure knowledge that the rest of her Idara is empowered to act in her stead.

So, over generations, have the Adelhardts assembled an array of territories and properties that is the envy of the other Idara.

After twenty minutes or so, the shuttle drops into normal space, and Paula swings about to watch the viewscreen, suddenly reminded of the reason she's returned to the Empire.

Outside, the shape of an enormous warbird looms dark against heavily-spread stars.

The present Imperial Eagle is the third flagship Maj Thovold has owned. The first of the line was a nothing, a shell constructed after the founding of the Empire as accessory to a throne that no one believed would ever be occupied. When Maj declared herself Empress (or was so declared by the Imperial Council; accounts differed), she had constructed a new flagship, keeping only the name and shape of the original. The third Eagle replaced the second after Maj dealt rather harshly with an uprising on Gotlan.

Whatever its precursors had been, the present Imperial Eagle is most impressive. It is the shape of a predatory eagle, wings spread a full hundred meters, talons poised seemingly ready to dismember any enemy ship or world. The Eagle's beak gleams of polished dellsite, its eyes hold laser cannon that can punch through asteroids. Space around the great ship is suffused with the summer-haze of her low-level defense screens—upon attack those screens energize fully, enveloping the ship in a protective cocoon of black, a cocoon which parts only when her powerful guns fire.

A docking bay open between the Eagle's legs, and Paula's shuttle slides smoothly into place. Pauls's pilot is steady; the shuttle experiences no difficulty and in only a few minutes Paula cycles the airlock and is met by the Empress' autoservants.

The servs escort her to an audience room halfway up the Eagle's neck. One whole wall of the room is a viewscreen that looks out onto the bridge. Paula feels the strong presence of the Admiral-that-was, rather than the Empress-who-is.

Maybe there is no distinction between the two.

"Sayyid Paula, please sit down."

Paula bows, kisses Maj's hand, then takes the proffered seat. Maj wears full Navy uniform—by far her most preferred dress —along with the Spiral and Six Globes Pendant that is reserved for the use of the sovereign. Another example, Paula thinks, of a ceremonial object whose creators had never expected to be used.

"You're wondering why I asked you to make your report here, rather than on Terra." The Empress gives Paula no chance to reply. "I am in the area checking out…well, things. If you had to travel through the Galaxy to Terra, I'd have to wait another two days for your report. I decided to save us both time by meeting you here."

"I am grateful, your Highness."

Maj waves a hand impatiently. "Forget that foolishness. You can't be grateful. I know you wanted to come to Terra, for the fleshpots of L4 if nothing else. Nevertheless, I'm sending you back to Tarantula without leave."

Paula allows disappointment to show on her face. It does no good, merely leaves her feeling silly with a ridiculous expression.

"Sayyid, please make your report. Seventy-five days ought to have given you enough time to observe the facility and come to some conclusions. What do you think of Tarantula?"

"May I speak freely, Highness?"

"For the stars'—da!"

"Tarantula disgusts me. I think it a travesty." She takes a deep breath. There, it is said, now maybe the rest will be easier.

Maj raises an eyebrow. "Do you care to elaborate?"

Paula leans forward in her seat. "To begin with, there are the physical conditions under which those people live. Scarcity of resources, hunger, sometimes even oxygen starvation. The entire system is programmed against them before they arrive, and they then have to survive in spite of the odds."

"I wasn't aware that most of them were dying."

"They're not. But at what a cost!" Paula waves in the general direction of the bridge's forward viewscreen. "Up there people live like savages. Let me tell you just one thing that happened to me.

"A tenday ago I was making an inspection trip to the habitable volume nearest the star Chi Rapere. The instant I left my ship I was besieged by about ten youngsters, the oldest about sixteen or so. At first I didn't understand what they wanted of me; it's hard to talk to people there unless you have radioes or can get into an atmosphere volume.

"I tried to get these young ones to follow me to the nearest atmosphere-bearing volume, but they wouldn't come. So I dragged them into the ship.

"As soon as the airlock closed they had taken off their helmets and were on the deck at my feet. Swearing loyalty and begging me not to hurt them, each one. I gave each to the charge of one of my officers, and I took the youngest one to my suite to get some sense from him. He was a boy of about twelve.

"His name, he told me, was Hamlin. As long as he could remember, he'd lived in nearby nodules, moving from one to another with his family as each node's atmosphere became unbreathable. The others in the ship were also children of his family, which seemed to have consisted of about twenty adults.

"A few days earlier—I could never work out the exact chronology, since these people have no means of telling time—another bunch of adults had come into the volume. There was a fight, and Hamlin's people were mostly killed. The youngest children were taken by the newcomers, but those with Hamlin had been set out on the Web as punishment for resisting takeover. They were told that they would be readmitted to atmosphere when they consented to become servants of the victors.

"Some gave in—Hamlin's older brother among them. After a while the brother returned with tales of cruelty that would make you shiver."

"I doubt it. I have a strong stomach. Comes from sitting in on too many Imperial Council meetings."

"Highness, this is hardly a joking matter. I'm talking about physical cruelty and mental degradation. Hamlin carefully explained to me that some of the members of his band were injured and could not be moved, so they had been eking out an existence by raiding the atmosphere volume for air and scouring the Web for food. If I hadn't arrived, they wouldn't have lasted another three days."

"So naturally you rescued them."

"I called for a ship to take them to a totally unexplored part of the Web, where they could be alone in peace."

"And the…I suppose 'pirates' is the word?"

"We broke up that atmosphere volume, took the pirates and scattered them one at a time through a billion cubic kilometers. I doubt they'll cause anyone trouble."

Maj twists a gold signet ring on her left hand. "I presume that this Hamlin episode is just one of many that you could regale me with."

"There are worse tales, Majesty."

"You must remember, Sayyid Paula, that you are administering a prison. What did you expect? You attended Harvard Leikeis—don't I remember that you took high marks in penal history?"

Paula draws back. "Your Highness, to study about such things centuries ago is one thing—to witness them in person today is a disgrace."

Maj Thovold settles back in her chair, closes her eyes, and sighs. For a moment, just a moment, Paula sees her as a woman rather than a ruler. The Empress' face is furrowed with age-lines, her hair wispy and white. There is a hint of a tic at the right corner of her dry lips.

Eyes still closed, Maj speaks softly. "What would you have me do with Tarantula?"

"Empress, I recommend that you close down the facility at once and recall all prisoners."

"And what should I do with them then?"

"Psych-adjustment worked for years before you took command of the Empire. And there are always new colonies to send less violent criminals."

The eyes snap open; Paula is reminded of the main guns of the Imperial Eagle. "And do you suppose conditions are much better on the colonies?"

"At least people can breathe."

"You may have a point. Now suppose I accept your recommendation and begin psych-conditioning the prisoners. What am I to do when the Council calls me to task for unfairly influencing the minds of those criminals?"

"You need merely explain that the prisoners are better off being conditioned, than they were in Tarantula." Without giving Maj time to come up with a counter-argument, Paula continues. "Besides, there's the matter of the Web itself. Its frontiers are propagating at a good fraction of lightspeed. The thing is getting completely out of control."

Maj nods, punches a few instructions on a keypad. Paula can't see the result.

"Is there nothing good about Tarantula? Only unrelieved misery and cruelty?"

"Of course not. There are good people, and some portions of the Web have even made a good deal of progress. I wouldn't hesitate to call them civilized. Why, one leader, a certain Tsung-Dao Wu, has managed to make a good life for the people under his control."

Again the keypad, and the Empress gives a little smile. "Yes, Tsung-Dao. He was quite a troublemaker."

"I'm not surprised. I've spoken with him; he you and your rule in poor regard."

"So now Tsung-Dao is a leader among people, a very productive fellow. Back in the Empire, he'd once again be a dangerous radical. I'd have to step in and send him off to a new colony...in which case he'd return five years later with an army...or have him conditioned. And I've no doubt that conditioning would destroy whatever good there is in the man. Which would you have me choose, Sayyid Paula?"

Paula remains silent.

"You see, my Sayyid, in a sense Tarantula is a new colony. One of the strangest we have, granted, but I hope that in a few generations it will contribute a lot to the Empire. Do I have the right to step in and alter the course of their development?"

"I would ask, rather, if you have the right to ignore them. I say not." Paula's heart pounds, and her muscles are tense with adrenalin.

"Sayyid, I think your report is done. I will not cancel the Tarantula project right away. I will take your recommendations under consideration, and shall have some decisions for you shortly. Meanwhile...."

"Meanwhile I have to sit by and watch people in misery, because you're running some political experiment!" Now she's done it. It was not a good idea to lose one's temper in the presence of the Empress. Well, time to go all the way. "Just what do you think gives you the power to meddle in people's lives to such an extent?"

The Empress' response is calm, her voice tired. "I have the power, Paula Adelhardt, because I took it. I keep it because no one can stop me." Maj reaches out at hand to Paula; Paula ignores it. "Go back to Tarantula. Help Tsung-Dao and the others like him to build a society out there. And…if you can… trust me. "

Paula can take no more. The colossal arrogance of the woman! She turns and deliberately strides out of the audience chamber, her autoservant guide flying at full speed to catch up. Back in her shuttle, she watches the Imperial Eagle recede and tastes anger and disappointment.

Tsung-Dao is right. Absolute power over a Galaxy of two trillion people is too much for any one person to bear alone.

What to do about it?

VI.
"This ghastly, thin-faced time of ours"
Taratula Nebula, Large Magellanic Cloud
Thursday, 5 April TE 219

Water swirls about Tsung-Dao, and he gives thought to cliches about the endless adaptability of Humankind.

Humanity didn't need the Web to prove its ability to adapt. Even before Tarantula, any number of worlds had aquatic populations. Tsung-Dao remembers reading about the planet T Keimai, where Human colonists opted for gengineering that would permit their descendants to live underwater naturally. Given the physical structure of the Web, it was inevitable that some group would stumble upon a water-filled atmosphere volume and attempt to live in it. After all, a vacuum suit's rebreather didn't care where it got its oxygen reserve; and edible parts of the Web were common, water or no.

Inevitable or not, it was quite a surprise to find such a volume only a few billion kilometers from his home.

The Elder is speaking again; Tsung-Dao strains his concentration to follow the man's rapid hand movements, all the while keeping a steady counterpoint with the handsign for "repeat."

"We are happy here," the Elder signs. "I see not, why we ought to help your group."

He wishes he knew the sign for a sigh. "We can work together for our—" Damn, what"s the sign for mutual? —"shared benefit. You are old enough to remember the Empire; do you not desire the benefits of civilization?"

"I was sent away from the Empire because I opposed a woman who tried to take away our freedom to be what we desire. My family was prosperous, then she removed our fortune when she assumed control of the marketplace. So I was sent here. Now my children and others of my group live the way they wish, with no unhappiness. We are prosperous once again. We have food, we have air, we have pressure to keep us from exploding. What more do we want?"

"We can offer you computers, access to starships, all the conveniences of trade."

Beneath the helmet of his vacuum suit the man's eyes narrow. "Once I fought a tyrant who tried to force me under her rule—now I think perhaps I face another. You are not welcome here, sire. Please leave."

"You have granted me hospitality. At least let me —"

"Tsung-Dao, please go." The Elder lays a hand on Tsung-Dao's shoulder, and suddenly Tsung-Dao is once more a young man of eighteen facing his first session in the Imperial Council, and finding friendship from one of the older delegates....

Hand-motions fail him; he can only whisper, "Y-you're Edward Engelbach."

"If you feel that you owe me any loyalty or friendship, or just the common decency that was once the rule between Idara —then please, Tsung-Dao, leave me to the path I have chosen."

"But Syyid Edward, you—" No. There are a thousand people in this pod; he can't hope to stand against them. Without a word or sign, he lets two younger ones lead him to the airlock, then he plunges through a series of sphincters into vacuum.

Far-off and indistinct, streamers of the Web are faint smears against the white of the Nebula.

Three hundred meters away is an Imperial starboat. And his own starship is nowhere to be seen. Good crew.

From behind Web-strands, the meter-high form of a cyborg drifts into view. Tsung-Dao turns on his suit radio with a quick motion. "Drav Lokys. Imagine meeting you here."

The cyborg drifts closer. "Even after ten years here I'm still amazed at the variety that obtains in Tarantula." One of Drav's waldoes gestures to the atmosphere pod behind Tsung-Dao. "Do they really live underwater all the time?"

"Except when they have to leave to search for more food or the makings of a vacuum suit. We've had them under observation for a while; it was only now that I was able to get out here to ask them to join our confederation."

The lens of Lokys' camera spins as the instrument focuses on Tsung-Dao's face. "How did you get out here, Tsung-Dao Wu?" Is the suspicious tone in the cyborg's voice only Tsung-Dao's imagination?

"We have spaceships, Drav Lokys. You've seen our launch systems yourself. Kerosene and oxygen are easy enough to get, and they provide quite a kick of acceleration."

"I can imagine. How did you expect to get back to your base?"

"A larger ship will be following me." Tsung-Dao made certain that his home maintained their rocket industry for local trade within a few billion kilometers—absence of long-range transport would make the Imperials suspicious.

"Well, we can't wait for it. Sayyid Paula requests that you join her."

"Sayyid Paula presumes upon my valuable time."

"Don't be an ass. What she sees in you I don't know, but she wants you to have dinner with her and I've been told to fetch you as soon as possible. If you don't want to keep seeing her, that's a matter for you to explain in person."

"Sure." He follows Drav Lokys to the Imperial boat, a five-meter, ten-passenger standard model. He and Lokys are the only occupants..

Perhaps, Tsung-Dao thinks, this is the time to have a serious talk with Paula Adelhardt. She is a nice woman, somewhat simple but pleasant enough to be with. He enjoyed the talks they've had, lingering over large dinners lit only by candles and the Nebula itself. Still, at least part of the reason he keeps seeing her is to report to Masayyid Brin and Catherine. Is that fair to her?

It isn't as if he can possibly have any romantic interest in her. She is nothing but a minor chip in the vast Imperial machinery, like hundreds of other Idara back in the Milky Way. Once, he thought he would be fated, by political necessity, to mate with one of those women—luckily destiny saved him from that sentence. Upper-class fluffs, all of them.

Sure, Paula opposed the Empress—in a minor way, while still accepting Maj's authority and granting her the right to rule. As long as Paula held her assumptions unquestioned, Tsung-Dao could never take her quite seriously.

Before Tsung-Dao is ready, Drav flickers the boat through tachyon phase and Imperial Headquarters looms on the viewscreen. There is enough starship traffic in this region to keep the volume free of Web-strands; Imperial Headquarters floats alone, an improbable, roughly cone-shaped jumble of life-modules and support struts, docking bays and storage volumes. Tsung-Dao recognizes it as a standard Imperial Station Class 4-I.

Every other time Paula's had him brought here, the viewscreens were blanked. Why? Is she ashamed to parade Imperial wealth before the poor prisoner who struggles for his daily air ration? Then why isn't she ashamed of the sumptuous meals she has served right from the station's foodsynth?

"I've never seen Imperial Headquarters before," he comments.

Drav's cameras don't turn from the boat's controls. "Sayyid Paula suffers from the aristocracy's fixation with security."

"Whereas you, on the other hand, don't consider me a security risk?"

"On the contrary. I've just followed your career long enough that I know you have no reason or desire to attack Imperial Headquarters. You've washed your hands of the Empire; you don't want to be reminded that we exist."

"You presume quite a bit, Drav Lokys." The curving wall of the station slides past and autoservants emerge to lock on a docking tunnel. Drav shuts down the boat's systems and moves toward the airlock. "You're right. I presume. I got curious about you, Tsung-Dao Wu. Once you were Sayyid Tsung-Dao and coming up for a position of leadership in a very powerful Idara. You threw it all away to lead a silly revolt against the Empress, a revolt which was sloppy to begin with and pathetic in the end. Then, when you were tried and sentenced to one of the new colonies, you went out of your way to insult the magistrate so you would be exiled to Tarantula instead."

"You've done thorough research." They stand before the airlock; neither presses the button that would open it. Tsung-Dao feel's Drav's cameras on him as if they are living eyes. "And from all this you conclude that I'm not a security risk?"

"'The Empire doesn't interest you. If it did, you would be there now. Instead, you're here—and you've built up the most worthwhile and prosperous society in this entire Galaxy." Drav's synthetic voice drops. "I don't know, if someone came along and offered you a foolproof plan to overthrow the Empress, maybe you'd go along with it. But I think after a while you would begin to doubt and wonder."

Tsung-Dao fights the impulse to stiffen, forces himself to relax. His thoughts bound wildly...has Drav Lokys been playing with him? Even now, does a squad of Imperial Marines wait on the other side of the airlock, to take him for drugging, questioning, punishment?

Drav touches the button, the airlock door slides open and reveals...nothing but the empty docking bay. Tsung-Dao's lips quiver in a smile, but he gives no other sign of his relief.

The Imperials are stupid, all of them, they don't know what's going on under their own viewscreens.

"She's waiting for you," Drav tells him. "You know the way." Watching the cyborg retreat into the ship, Tsung-Dao hears as if by tape-delay Drav's last words in his mind: "...you would begin to doubt and wonder."

Maybe they aren't as stupid as he thinks.

VII.
"Her soul's screen"
Tarantula Nebula, Large Magellanic Cloud
Thursday, 5 April TE 219

"She is stupid, Catherine. Stupid. You are much too subtle."

Datascreens, all alight with glowing letters and numbers, reports from a double-dozen operatives, surround Sayyid Catherine Leonov. She gestures to them. "You underestimate her. Stupid she is not, Brin. One does not advance to the highest position in the Galaxy, then reign in that position for over thirty years, by being stupid. Maj Thovold is subtle, the most subtle opponent we have ever faced." She puts her fingertips together and glanced again at one of her reports.

"The idea," Brin continues, "Is to get her to come to us. Look at her—she quests about like a tracker without a scent. She has missed your little hints, my love. Missed them entirely. She will never pick up the trail unless we give her something more definite."

Catherine closes her eyes. Impatience—another sign of her husband's too-quick decline. She lets out a sigh, then calmly turns to him. "No, she has not missed my hints. She knows, knows that we are here. She even knows it is us. She may not realize it, but down where it counts, down where her mind makes its decisions, she is certain." Her eyes focus on his face. "What would you have me do, Husband? Do you want me to be so blatant that her damned Terrad computers will read the traces and tell her all about our plans? Were I that obvious, she would know at once that this is a trap."

"We have worked on this for decades. We cannot wait much longer."

No, my husband, it is you who cannot wait longer. It is you who has lost your drive, lost the vision that should sustain you. I should not wonder, that vision is strong enough to burn out any lesser soul. "I will wait as long as I must, but I will see her dead at my hands." Catherine flexes the strong muscles of her arms. Native flesh and implants, she is healthy enough to live…to live as long as she wished.

"Maj Thovold will come to us, Brin. She will come unsuspecting, underestimating us. The years will have blurred her memory of what we can do. She will not believe that we can possibly be so patient as to release only those clues she needs to find us. She will think us careless, unable to hide ourselves. She will think us not in control of the situation. And so she will come, and she will be surprised to find that our control is absolute. I have planned this trap for thirty years, Brin. Trust me, it will work."

"I suppose you know what is right."

"Yes, I do." Pity. Once he would have argued with her, if he thought he was right. Once, he might even have changed her mind. That is all gone now; she is left with only an ordinary man.

Just as well. There is no part in coming events for him. There will be room for only one pair of hands around Thovold's throat, only one set of senses to drink her dying agony, one pair of lips to give voice to laughter….

IX.
"And when your veins were void and dead"
New York, Terra
Monday, 12 April TE 219

From her Palace window Maj looks out under the dome of Manhattan on the massive bureaucratic mausoleum of the Imperial State Building. A creation of the first optimistic decades of Empire, over two centuries the building grew and digested neighboring structures like a megalomaniac amoeba. Luckily, reorganization of the Empire stopped its growth, else all Terra might now be nothing but the headquarters of the Empire's civil servants.

She gathers her robes about her. Robes! They are as comfortable as she can make them, but there is a limit to comfort when one costume must fit the formal styles of every planet under her command. Most of the lines of the Imperial Dress Robes, like the Spiral Crown, were designed by symbol-minded Idara to be displayed in a museum. In her darker moods, she wonders if the Dress Robes are nothing but the Imperial Council's revenge.

The Hall of the Council is a short subway trip away. Careless of hems dragging on the floor, Maj strides through her maximum-security entrance, pauses for a second to check the time, then walks out into full view of the Council.

She looks out over the heads of all two-hundred-one delegates, over the Visitor's Gallery, past clouds of hovering autoservants awaiting their respective masters' orders. The Hall is well-lit; she has no trouble finding what she wants. It greets her like an old friend. Shining on the back wall of the Hall in multicolor figures is the display of a very special clock. This clock, set counting at the very instant the Empire was proclaimed, has ticked off each and every second between then and now.

Maj has measured out her life against that clock. Its digits marked the second she received her commission in the

Imperial Navy, the hour she was promoted to Supreme Admiral, the day she became Secretary-General. It marked the instant she took a Throne which had been vacant since its creation. The clock counted her every tangle with the Council, ticked through every reform that passed, comforted her in the face of each new setback. Under the figures of that clock Maj grew old, older than anyone had a right to be. After she was dead, if she were lucky, that clock would continue through the centuries, marking each separate second of the existence of the Terran Empire.

If she were lucky. And if she did her job right.

This instant the clock says 6,915,205,177. Then -8. Then -9.

She raises the scepter, cursing the angle of light that sends flashes stabbing into her eyes off diamond facets. "Members of the Imperial Council, I stand before you as first among equals." Ha! Ridiculous formula…but the Council insisted. And in these inconsequential symbolic matters, Maj always let them have their way. "Why have you summoned me?"

Ross Carroll pulls himself to his feet and totters a few steps forward. As long as a Carroll sits in the Council to represent Idara Carroll—which only happens when Idara Carroll can agree on a single representative, a truly rare occurrence—then the scion of this highest-ranking Idara speaks for the Council. Maj hopes Ross won't serve much longer…it takes him minutes to complete even the most simple statement, and once he actually dozed off in the middle of an address.

"Your Highness, we in the Council are very concerned about the results of your latest physical examination."

I'm a damned site healthier than you, old fool, Maj thinks.

"The galaxy is…er…painfully aware that you have not yet designated your successor."

Maj leans forward. "What you mean is that you're afraid I'm going to keel over, and you'll have to fight it out yourselves to see who gets to replace me."

"Her Majesty is being…ah…blunt. We fear that there will be unrest should you go to your Ancestors, before you have told us who will replace you."

"My provisional choice of a successor is on file with the Terrad system. If I die, Terrad has orders to release it. And only if I die." Bluff, bluff. The only name in Terrad's file is one she never intends to share, a rotten choice for Emperor with the sole redeeming feature of being a complete nonentity, a perfect figurehead for whomever won the power struggle.

"Your Majesty, we can hardly be content with the assurance of sealed orders and mysterious last wishes. Surely you do not wish to see this Empire thrown into a violent civil conflict?"

Would serve you right, she thinks. That's how I found you, poised at the edge of war, Idara against Idara. If you haven't learned anything in all this time, why should I make it any easier for you once I'm gone?

The faces in the Visitor's Gallery catch her eye. Because of them. The poor little people, caught between and trod upon by the rulers. Trod upon—piffle! They are the spineless ones who never stand up to anyone trying to tread upon them. Even so, they deserve a life spared of the necessity to knuckle under to the biggest guns.

Time for bluff and bravado. "I will name a successor." Four hundred eyes are suddenly fixed upon her—Karin Chlad, as usual, is asleep in her seat. "In one tenday I will stand before you and announce my choice to succeed me. I, Maj Thovold, Empress of all the Terran Empire, have spoken." In a swirl of robes she turns her back upon them and strides out of the chamber.

Terrad is ready for her even as she boards the Imperial Subway Car. (There once was a time, Maj thinks, when she was able to go through an entire day without having her every convenience celebrated and deified. It is all to impress the commoners: the Imperial Bed, the Imperial Dining Table for the Imperial Breakfast, even the Imperial Toilet—with replicas of each on sale in all the better shops. And so on, through the day.)

•Maj,• Terrad says, •if you will allow us to be frank, what did you mean by that display?•

"They got on my nerves. I had to tell them something, or else they would have turned it into another attempt to take away my power to appoint my own successor." Of all her Imperial powers and prerogatives, this is the one Maj most firmly defended from the Council's encroachments. Let them tell her what to wear, what to say, where to live...but she demands the right to choose who will take over from her.

•Whom do you intend to name a tenday from now?•

"I wish I knew. Demn, I'm sick of this." The car arrives back at the Palace; she bounds up a dropshaft to the Imperial Bedroom and starts peeling off her robes. A glance at displays tells her that her advisors are waiting outside...well, let them wait.

Terrad's voice follows her up the shaft. •Don't you have any ideas?•

"I know who I don't want. I can't name any of them—if I give the nod to any one of the Idara, the rest will start fighting today, and never mind waiting until I'm dead. And to space with all the work I've done." Demn, demn, demn. If only she could remove all these old-guard conservatives from the Imperial Council. Then, with younger people in charge, people who grew up with her way of doing things....

Impossible. The Imperial Council is old. In all other sectors of the government, all hereditary administrative posts, was able to institute reform. Now an office-holder resigns when her successor reaches age 25. But a Council seat is an elected, not hereditary, right; and while the wise Councillors of a third-century ago had found it politically correct to pass the Empress' reforms in other areas, their tolerance did have limits. And despite the overwhelming majority of non-Idara seats in the Council, it is the Idara who make policy. So the Imperial Council remains old, with an average age this session of seventy-three.

"Who was behind this latest move?" she asks Terrad.

•A coalition. Chen, d'Herelle, Lütken, Elendan, Carcopino, Horlamus, McCaffrey, and Lei. The Schmidt Foundation and General Electronics. A few others of no account.•

"And who started it?"

•We have no information.•

"Guess." Oh, why couldn't they come up with a computer that could intuit? Terrad was the best, and yet it still refused to take the leap of faith, the necessary flash of co-ordination between unrelated events....

Lütken?

Tarantula?

Maj smiles. "Never mind. I don't need you to guess. I've come to a conclusion." She punches orders into the keyboard set in the wall next to her sleep cocoon—full holo recording, authentication codes, message to depart via spacemail courier for Tarantula Nebula.

The terminal beeps to tell her it is recording. Maj puts on her stern face. "To Sayyid Paula Adelhardt, Administrator of the Empire's Tarantula Nebula Facility, from her Empress. Greetings, Sayyid Paula. Since our last talk I have been thinking over what you told me about the Facility. I am still in deep consideration of your suggestions, but I feel a need to keep the situation from getting out of hand. Therefore, please begin immediate operations to limit the growth of the Web to its present dimensions. I will instruct Imperial biotechs to start studying the possibility of reversing the Web's growth.

"Your proposal of shutting down the Tarantula Facility permanently is being considered. I praise you for your concern over this matter, and I invite you to come to Terra at your earliest convenience to testify before an inquiry board. Your aggressive search for the facts of the Tarantula Facility is to be complimented.

"I, Maj Thovold, Empress of all the Terran Empire, have spoken."

Comp signals that the recording is on its way to a standby Imperial Navy ship that can reach the Greater Magellanic Cloud in only a day.

•And what,• says Terrad, •was that intended to accomplish?•

"We're going to have to make our plans very carefully from this point on," Maj answers. "Very carefully indeed."

•Is that what we asked?•

Maj only smiles.

IX.
"Where death must win"
Tarantula Nebula, Large Magellanic Cloud
Tuesday, 13 April TE 219

Brin Lütken has his comps keep a constant lookout for Imperial messages. By this time, it is habit—Brin always keeps an eye on what his enemies are doing. That is one of the reasons he has managed to stay alive so long.

The computer interrupts him with a report while he is busy with his collection. Although he is no longer able to use most of the thousands of weapons he has collected, he is still enormously proud of the assemblage. There are the obvious knives, swords, guns, and bombs…and more subtle pieces like vials of lethal viruses developed by Imperial biotechs; normal-looking personal datapads programmed to kill by giving fraudulent answers at the worst possible moment; a dinner jacket whose fibers grow together with monofilament strength, making death a crushing race between compression and suffocation. There are thousands of others, and Brin knows them all with the encyclopedic familiarity of the true hobbyist. This collection has followed him through the Empire and across intergalactic space; recently he has spent more time than ever going over it.

The computer's voice summons him; he slaps a contact on the side of his chair. "What is it?"

•An Imperial Navy ship just came out of tachyon phase fifty parsecs from the border of the Greater Cloud.•

"They deliver an ultrawave message. Find it."

There is a brief pause. The Empire routinely uses millions of different ultrawave frequencies; no instrument in the universe could possibly be versatile enough to attune to all of them. All Brin's equipment can do is scan the few dozen freqs most likely to be utilized by the Tarantula Facility.

•Message found. Record-delay broadcast commencing.•

In the air before him, Maj Thovold's image takes form. Brin listens as she barks orders to Paula Adelhardt, then sits for a moment, thinking. He touches a finger to the soft spot above his left clavicle; the touch activates Brin's oldest implant, a sealed-beam ultrawave transceiver linked to its identical twin in his wife's body. "Catherine?"

"Yes?"

"Get the computer to play Thovold's latest message for you." Over the circuit he hears a faint echo of the Empress' voice.

"Well?" she says.

"We cannot allow her to start dismantling the Web."

He can imagine Catherine's frown. "What do you have in mind?"

"It is obvious. If Paula Adelhardt is destroyed, then a new Liaison will be appointed. One with less radical ideas." Their parties in the Council will see to that.

"Catherine, let me do her." Brin runs his fingers over the nap of the dinner jacket…creative, but it has been done before. Perhaps this one: a gift box of cosmetics that react with perspiration to form a catalyst, turning human skin impermeable, closing up pores and slowly solidifying fatty deposits. Or….

"Maj Thovold expects us to try to kill the Adelhardt."

"Of course." What does Catherine think he is, simple? "And she expects us to realize that, and not make a move. Come, Catherine, you wanted some bait to draw her here. This will suffice, nyet?"

"Hmmm. Let me consider." Her voice takes on a faraway quality, and Brin knows she is in the room with no name, knows she is at least partially linked to the Web. Faraway? He suddenly looks at the bare Webstuff visible on the viewscreen, black against cloudy white. Is Catherine there? Does her presence surround their hidden base? Could he but reach out beyond dellsite wall and touch something that would convey its sensation to her? Is it imagination, or do the Web strands seem to quiver a bit?

"You are right, Brin. But not right enough. I cannot let you kill her."

"Confound it, Catherine...."

"No, you will like this better. We need her to bait our adversary, you said. Very well. We shall go all the way with it. Call Tsung-Dao Wu, and tell him to bring her to the appointed place. You know where I mean. That will surely bring Maj Thovold to investigate."

"She does not know that you control the Web. Is it wise to tip your hand so soon?"

This time he distinctly feels Catherine's smile. "No matter what, Maj Thovold will come. And this way—this way, she will be anticipating our attack. Is that not delicious?"

Brin puts the cosmetic case away on its shelf. There will be more use for it later. Catherine is right. It is so much sweeter, this way.

He closes the ultrawave link, and directs the computer to locate Tsung-Dao Wu.

XI.
"The vine's wet green"
Tarantula Nebula, Large Magellanic Cloud
Tuesday, 13 April TE 219

It was Tsung-Dao's idea; Paula could not refuse. Besides, a visit to his home-volume would be exciting. The worst thing about duty at Tarantula is being out of touch with the Empire: no holodramas, no news reports, no parties, and no companionship other than the hundred or so techs at the Imperial Headquarters. And the same faces, day after repetitive day.

So here she is, crouching in an atmosphere nodule, breathing air at one-third the pressure she is accustomed to, anchored to a springy Webstuff wall with too-flimsy tethers. Tsung-Dao crouches beside her, and at least fifty other people are scattered throughout the too-small volume. Luminous strands of Webmaterial, mixed in one of Tsung-Dao's factories, provide dim light—raw Web-protein, flavored and treated by a primitive food-synth, made a rather appetizing dish reminiscent of seafood.

"They call you Clanna," she says, gesturing to the people. "Is that a name, or a title?"

"A little of both. We have a loose clan structure here, nothing like the Idara in the Empire, but you have to understand that most of us grew up back home. They call me the leader of all clans." He laughs. "In the Empire, I guess the equivalent rank would be Planetary Governor."

"More like Emperor, I would think."

Frown. "Let's say Secretary-General, and leave it at that."

She remembers how much he hates the Empress, hates the whole concept of allowing someone—anyone—to occupy the Throne. Tsung-Dao is a real rebel, a child of the generation before hers. If she had any courage, Paula suddenly thinks, she too would be doing as he does, facing exile rather than betraying his beliefs.

Of course, Maj's latest message might mean an end to all that. Maybe Paula has finally convinced her that Tarantula is evil....

She gestures at the people surrounding them. "You've done such great things here, starting with so little. Reactors, factories, agriculture, rapidtrans systems, relativistic spaceships—my mind reels."

"It hasn't been easy, and I haven't done it alone. Everyone here works ten hours out of twenty, and still it's taken us decades to build what little we have. Probably centuries before we can export our technology to the rest of the Web." He frowns. "It hasn't been our sole doing." He leans forward, coming closer to her than he ever has, and for a moment Paula is afraid he's going to kiss her. "Paula, we've had help. And now They want to meet you."

They? She feels a jolt. Exiled Imperial scientists and techs? A previously undiscovered alien race? Computer remnants of some long-vanished culture native to the Magellanic Clouds?

"Who are...They?"

"I'm not allowed to tell you. But I am permitted to take you there." Tsung-Dao bites his lower lip.

"All right. I'll have the ship—"

"No. They said I was to come alone with you. Listen, Paula, I know I'm not making sense. Believe me, I wouldn't do this if I didn't have orders from Them. You'll just have to trust me."

For a moment she remembers penology classes, the endless recitations of neuroses and psychoses that struck prison populations. But Tarantula is no normal prison, Tsung-Dao no normal man.

"Fine. We can take one of the ship's lifeboats. I can pilot well enough to take us where we're going." She narrows her eyes. "Where are we going? Inside the Cloud?"

"Inside the Nebula. Another part of the Web."

"Should be no trouble. As long as you're not willing to tell me what this is all about—"

"Not able, Paula."

"Whichever. When do we leave?"

"'As soon as we're done eating, if you want."

She pops one more morsel into her mouth, grateful for the Imperial Headquarters food-synth. A steady diet of this stuff would be too much. "I'm finished."

Paula is no master-pilot; she lets the autopilot do most of the work and only interrupts it for fine-tuning details. The heading Tsung-Dao gives her is a string of numbers that locate a specific spot in the Imperial three-dimensional grid that had been set up for the Greater Magellanic Cloud; she has no difficulty finding the particular spot of the Web.

The tiny boat comes out of tachyon phase, a dull jerk echoes through cabin grav, then a larger jolt as Webstuff tears away and a patch of Nebula-light fades on the rear viewscreen.

They are in magic-land.

At first her only impression is of arching Web-stuff with sparks of electric blue racing along them. Like a winter forest against a stormy sky, branches of the Web reach in all directions, interlacing and forming a freeform pattern that changes as the boat races through it.

Instruments reveal that they are within an atmosphere volume—an immense one. Ladar imaging reveals the far wall several kilometers distant. Ambient pressure is about one-quarter standard, and instruments show a bit too much nitrogen for comfortable breathing. There is nothing corrosive or poisonous in this atmosphere; vacuum suit respirators will suffice for EVA gear.

The hole their boat made in the wall calmly but quickly sealed itself; there is an increase of electrical light in that area. Shadow-images play across a wall of Webstuff, and the hole winks shut. With an impact too gentle to feel, the boat hits a wall and sticks.

Paula turns her eyes on Tsung-Dao. "Where are They? " she whispers. She wonders if she is already in the presence of Them. Half-forgotten stories come back to her now...giant brains sleeping out in the cold of space, huge minds that dwarf humans'....

"They will be here. Perhaps we should go out and wait for Them."

She nods. Palm to the airlock, and it starts its cycle. She takes comfort from Tsung-Dao's body close to hers in the tiny airlock. Then he steps to the Web wall, and gives her a hand.

No need for tethers; the material of the Web wall is slightly tacky. The sensation is like stepping through mud, or like the anticrash fields that the big Imperial Navy ships have—it takes a conscious effort to walk.

Off to the right, a blue light blinks steadily. Tsung-Dao peers after it. "This way, I think."

Paula moves too quickly, loses her footing, and starts sailing away. Tsung-Dao snags her by an ankle and returns her to the Web. "Keep one foot in contact with the wall at all times," he cautions. "We should have brought safety lines. I didn't think we'd have to go so far. "

Onward they walk. For all the massive strands like tree trunks and the floor like detritus-covered mush, Paula thinks, this is not at all like walking through a forest on a planet. It is another place and another sort of experience altogether. Little pale shadows chase each other beneath her feet as sparks move along Web-branches.

"Tsung-Dao, I don't think that light is getting any closer."

"I don't either. This isn't like Them."

"Are you sure They know you were coming?"

"They said They would be waiting."

"Maybe we ought to return to the boat and…."

"And what?" The helmet radio removes some of the personality of his voice, leaving his words flat.

"Look at the boat." She feels him turn, but she can't take her eyes away. The starboat is not that far, less than five hundred meters at most. Then why does it look so indistinct, so foreshortened?

A particularly bright flash of light passes in front of the boat, and Paula gasps. Looping over and about the craft are dark tendrils of Webstuff, weaving purposefully like the longest snakes she's ever seen. Already the vessel's landing gear are completely covered, and the tendrils reach beyond the airlock on this side.

She takes off in a flying zero-grav leap. Tsung-Dao leaps after her, two meters behind.

From nowhere a brightly-glowing tendril of Web whips in front of her and strikes her across the shoulders. Where it hits, it hurts, and where it hurts it clings. Tsung-Dao sails past, unable to stop himself.

Paula reaches for her laser knife, trying to remain calm. Some sections of the Web, she had read, are genetically engineered to play the part of bacteria and break down the tissues of dead organisms, to transport needed trace minerals to other parts of the Web. Obviously they have stumbled on a mutated portion of the Web, a portion that doesn't know they aren't dead yet. A few blasts of laser light should free her, then together she and Tsung-Dao can board the boat and, and—

Too late. Her hands are both encased in charged ropes of light. More tendrils loop about her body; she can almost believe they are groping for her helmet, fumbling purposefully in search of latches.

Then Tsung-Dao is there, a Navy laser rifle from the boat's arms locker in his hand. A few shots, and Paula is detached from the main Web. The tendrils embracing her still have their motion, their obscene pseudo-life; but they have lost the nightmare aim and intent. A close shot, and she is able to free her hand; her own laser knife makes short work of cutting away the rest of her bonds.

She leaps for Tsung-Dao's arms. He pushes her in the direction of the ship and fires a few more blasts at Web-fingers waving in her direction.

The airlock is almost covered, although she can see burnt stumps where Tsung-Dao must have forced his way in. She fires her laser knife without care, knowing she can't harm the boat's dellsite skin; then she jumps in and gasps, settling her back against the airlock door as it closes satisfactorily.

After only a few seconds, Tsung-Dao is inside. Paula wastes no time triggering the boat's antigravs; before they are even strapped in the craft breaks through the node's wall and they are back amid Nebula-light, with the Web nothing more than an indifferent presence about them.

Paula sets course for Imperial Headquarters, knowing that something is dreadfully wrong.

XII.
"The die rang sideways as it fell"
Tarantula Nebula, Large Magellanic Cloud
Tuesday, 13 April TE 219

Why? Why? As they draw ever-closer to Imperial Headquarters, Tsung-Dao wonders in a world suddenly dropped on its head.

It was Masayyid Brin and Catherine. That much is self-evident. They told him where to take Paula, They did not show up, They tried to kill her...why?

The boat docks, and Tsung-Dao follows Paula to the station's master comm room. Numbly, he perches on a chair in a corner while Paula breathlessly gives orders to the comm officer.

Paula is not a bad person. Sure, her ideals are a bit fresh—but as life goes on they will become tattered about the edges, and soon she won't be a threat to anyone. Why did Catherine and Brin try to kill her? Do they seriously expect anything to come of her notion of shutting down Tarantula?

Paula slides into the comm officer's seat and consults directly with the base computer. "Scramble all ships—protective patrol. Dispatch special message courier at once to Terra, for the eyes of the Empress only. Message follows."

Why do They feel They need Paula out of the way? Their fleet is almost complete. Tarantula provided the people to crew the ships. All battle plans are drawn up, gone over endlessly with all available tacticians. From somewhere, Catherine produced three techs who'd worked with the Terrad system—a comparable set of computers constantly run simulations of the final attack against the Empire.

Suppose Tarantula were disbanded. Suppose Imperial ships converge on the Web and start evacuating prisoners? It wouldn't happen quickly; there would be plenty of time to strike, to topple the monarchy before it became hereditary, before all those who remember the old days are gone. Rule of Council, not Empress, is assured no matter what happens now.

So why are they so worried about Paula?

"Paula Adelhardt, Imperial Liaison to the Tarantula Facility, to Maj Thovold, Empress. Greetings, your Highness. I have just this instant returned from a very disturbing encounter with the Web."

Disturbing? Stars, Paula is still shaking. Tsung-Dao himself is frightened. He knows her manner, though—the manner of an Idara dealing with the incredible by reducing it in scope. Noblesse oblige, and Tsung-Dao was raised by the same code.

"At approximately seventeen hundred hours today, Tsung-Dao Wu and I were physically attacked by the Web. This attack was apparently unprovoked. It is my opinion that some guiding intelligence was behind the attack. Your Highness, something is very wrong with the Web—I suggest that we do not know all we need about it. I request that you send military reinforcements immediately along with a scientific team to completely investigate this matter."

Reinforcements. Scientific teams. And will they be sent?

And if they are…what will Catherine and Brin do to them? How many others might be hurt in the process? How many of his own people are in danger?

"Highness, I cannot recommend too strongly that this facility be closed down at once. When word of this accident leaks out—" she glances at the comm officer, who is busy looking elsewhere "—there will almost certainly be panic throughout Imperial Headquarters and probably the Web as well. We have a highly dangerous situation on our hands.

"If possible, I urge that you yourself come to Tarantula to oversee the operation."

Yes, noblesse oblige still lives. But something has vanished. Spirit. Faced with a crisis like this, an Idara of Tsung-Dao's time would have handled things herself, taken command. Paula's first action is to call for the Empress. Afraid of responsibility, all of them, and that is why the Empress held her post, would hold it until people like Catherine, Brin, and Tsung-Dao could—

Come to Tarantula?

Maj Thovold?

She will. She will have to. Paula isn't capable of commanding, there's no one else to take charge. The Empress has ultimate power, ultimate responsibility, and she does not delegate. Yes, she will come.

And...she will die.

At the hands of the Web. At the hands of Catherine and Brin.

Tsung-Dao's mind races. There is no rebellion plan after all. Fleet, personnel, years of machinations in the Empire and without, all a blind. The real goal is what Catherine said once before, apparently as a joke: to kill Maj Thovold.

He shivers. That means...that means they engineered the threat to Paula, tried to kill her simply to draw Maj here. And they allowed her to escape so that she would dictate this semi-hysterical message. They manipulated the Web, manipulated Paula, manipulated...him.

All their actions were calculated toward this very course. They took over the Web, and everyone in it danced to their commands. Without even knowing it.

Suddenly, the fleet that Catherine and Brin assembled here, so far beyond the stars of home, takes on a new and very sinister meaning. Maj Thovold took command of the Empire with the fleets of the Imperial Navy. Did Catherine and Brin learn from her example?

Knowing what he now knows of them...once the strike comes off, once an Empire in shock from the death of its leader is whipped into submission—will They then step down and give the Imperial Council ultimate power once again?

Or has Tsung-Dao merely been working toward trading one master for two others?

What should a man do, when he realizes that he has been fighting on the wrong side?

Wiping his cheeks dry without wondering when and how they became wet, Tsung-Dao stands and puts his hand on Paula's shoulder.

"Hold recording," she says, looking up at him. "What is it?"

"Tell the Empress that we know who's behind all this. It's Sayyid Brin Lütken and Sayyid Catherine Leonov. She'll know what to do."

He hopes.

XIII.
"After change of soaring feather"
New York, Terra
Wednesday, 14 April TE 219

Well, Ancestor, Maj thinks to the ghost that constantly follows her about these days, You're going to get to see the Magellanic Clouds up close.

Terrad is not pleased.

•It is unwise for you to leave the Galaxy now.•

"No more unwise than at any other time."

•We stand corrected. It is unwise for you to leave the Galaxy. No qualifications.•

"I don't see why you say that." Maj dresses herself in her best fighting uniform. No nonsense with Imperial regalia this trip. She has a job to do, a job she's waited three decades and more to finish. She has to push Maj Thovold, First Empress, aside for the duration, push her aside to make full room for Maj Thovold, Supreme Admiral. And Maj Thovold, Fighter.

Yet an arthritic tingle in her joints reminds her that she is not what she was. The Supreme Admiral has aged fantastically, the Fighter might be on her last legs.

Did I refuse, her Ancestor seems to berate her. When I was old as you are yourself, faced with open seas and unknown dangers, faced with flimsy canoes and hostile surrounding tribes, did I refuse? And my daughters, should they then refuse the challenges that come before them as they reach out to ever further islands?

•The situation in the Council is highly unstable. In six days you have promised to name a successor for them. What will they think if you now go rushing off to the Magellanic Clouds? What will they do when you are out of contact and they have free run of the Empire?•

"They will do nothing. They will spend their time arguing, bickering with one another, and getting nothing accomplished. Without my constant presence as a common enemy, they will disintegrate into factions just as their fathers and mothers did before I came along."

•We remind you that there is still a suspected usurpation plot to contend with.•

Gloves, helmet, and over her uniform a mirrored cape. Useful for deflecting stray laser shots. "I am going to deal with that usurpation. Catherine Leonov and Brin Lütken are behind it, and to end the plot I must confront them." She holds up a hand to silence the next objection. "Yes, I know that's just what they want me to do. So I will do it—but I will plan one step beyond that. One way or another, I have opposed these two for fifty years. I know how they think, and I'm prepared for them."

•You deal in levels of subtlety that are dangerous. Tsung-Dao Wu has informed you that they have a star fleet of respectable size—and our ships have been unable to locate that fleet. With you gone from the Empire, it will be a perfect time for their fleet to strike.•

"I have given you full authority to command the Navy. Admiral Mersand will follow all your orders, you know that. You can defend the Empire better than I can. But they won't attack. Not while I'm still alive. After I'm killed, in the confusion that's when they'll try to take over. Except that I won't be killed."

•And if you are?•

Maj smiles. If she is…but she won't be. It is not yet time for her to join her Ancestors.

•If you are killed…who will take your place?•

"Don't tell me you're still worried about that. That phase of this operation is over. The tenday deadline I gave myself in the hearing of the entire Empire—that was just an attempt to force their hands and make them move now. It worked." Sidearms, defense screen generator on her belt, power pack fully charged. Maj Thovold is as ready as any combat veteran. "Do you remember the campaign for Telorbat? That was my first command. The first time I acted under direct orders of Terrad."

•You exceeded your orders. You succeeded, and so we recommended you for decoration and promotion. Had you failed, a court-martial would have resulted.•

"I didn't fail."

•Condemn it, Maj, things are different. You are no longer Captain Thovold—you are Empress Thovold and you are the only thing that holds the Empire together. It is our job to defend this planet and the Empire. How can we do that if you run off and get yourself killed?•

"Would you rather have Catherine Leonov on the loose? I can stay at home, wait for her to move, and probably wrest this fleet away from her. Thirty years from now, fifty, eighty— she'll be back with another. And I'll have to be here to counter it." She gazes at the Imperial Robes hanging in her wardrobe. "I have no desire to live through the next ten decades carrying on a battle with Catherine Leonov like some figure in a blasted holoepic. Let it end now."

•You are Empress. The decision is yours to make.• There is a hesitation, and then, •Be glad you have that choice.•

"My decision is made. Let the Speaker of the Council play at being in charge for a while. I have a ship to catch."

Reed canoe or starship, it makes no difference. A ship to catch, a job to do. Maj leaves her room, and a long string of ghosts follow her.

XIV.
"If one should love you with real love"
Tarantula Nebula, Large Magellanic Cloud
Thursday, 15 April TE 219

Yes, Catherine thinks with joy, we still have our contacts, we still have our servants in the Empire. Maj Thovold may think she banished Sayyid Catherine Leonov from the Galaxy—let her learn too late how mistaken she was.

"You are sure," she says to the figure before her, "that the Empress left on her ship? You are certain this is not another feint?"

"We've had hourly reports from our agent on Imperial Eagle. Only by racing here in the fastest drones have his messages been able to reach us. She will be here, with her flagship fully crewed, in a matter of hours."

A smile tugs at the corners of Catherine's lips. Too soon to smile yet, too soon to anticipate victory. There is yet a long hard struggle ahead, feint and counter-feint, stroke and counterstroke, before Maj Thovold lies dead on this very floor. They will need their wits about them, for truly the real battle is only just beginning.

"Thank you." Catherine throws a small bag at her informer; he opens it and counts a starship's price in Imperial Dollars. "You are paid—go." At her words, the man before her turns, moves away...but before he has gone five meters he turns back. "Sayyid, I —"

He tumbles to the floor, rolls, and lies still. Catherine stands and slowly walks to the inert form.

"You thought you were safe, nyet? The chits, dalinka. Coated with a fast-multiplying virus. Feeds on superconductors. Destroys conductivity, you know—and without conductivity, you are nothing but a worthless lump." No use saying more—the paralyzed thing on the floor can no longer hear her. Even now, the brain inside has begun to starve for oxygen. Before long, it will be dead.

Catherine fetches a vial from her pocket and sprinkles its contents on the pile of machinery. This counter-virus will destroy all trace of the original.

For Drav Lokys, it is already far too late.

"Jettison this," she instructs a waiting autoservant, and settles back into her chair.

"Why did you do that?" Brin brings his chair around with a lurch. "He was one of our best operatives."

"He knew who and where we are. He was intelligent enough to figure out what we are doing. At this late date, I cannot permit any threats to remain." Why does he ask her this? Surely he knows the answer? Brin always knew, was always the one to suggest the drop of poison, the touch of lysin, the quick movement of the hands that brought oblivion and an end to bother.

"For gods' sakes, Catherine, he was conditioned. He could not have betrayed us if he had wanted to."

For a second she doesn't know what to say. Who is this stranger, who has taken control of her husband's body? What bizarre entity is using Brin's mouth to say these things? "Beloved, Maj Thovold can break conditioning. I will not take any chance of betrayal min the last hours of our scheme."

"I suppose it was necessary."

She looks after the autoservant, vanishing around a corner with its burden dragging. "Of course it was necessary."

He wheels his chair to face a viewscreen, looks out upon the Web. "I do not understand why you let Paula Adelhardt escape. I wanted that strumpet dead."

"I told you before, we needed her to summon Thovold." Husband, what have you become? Do you remember nothing, from one day to the next? Where is the mind that once stored all the details of a dominion that stretched across a Galaxy? Where is the memory that classified the desires, the weaknesses, the geeking thresholds of every member of the Imperial Council?

Brin, where have you gone?

And why now, when I need you the most?

"So she comes at last. After so many years, Maj Thovold is coming." He holds up a hand to the viewscreen, and Catherine struggles not to notice the tremor in that hand. "And we will be there to welcome her, da? Tell me again, Catherine, tell me what we will do to her."

Catherine stands behind her husband, her hands on his shoulders. They lower under her touch. "We will kill her, Brin. But first, we will make her suffer."

"Yes, make her suffer for all she has done to us." Brin puts his hand over hers, turns to look around the room. His collection of weapons iss all about, scattered in the organized clutter that is so familiar to her after so much time. She feels that she can fetch each weapon, identify where he got it, what they were doing when it was acquired. She knows each of them as intimately as she knows him.

No. Knew him.. This new creature, this failing wizened hulk, this is not her Brin.

He leans his head against her, and for the first time since they met, too many lifetimes ago, she feels a desire to recoil from his touch.

"Catherine...suppose she wins?"

Indignity of indignities! Brin never doubted. Even when everything toppled about them, when they raced for unknown stars with only their personal yacht and the Imperial Navy trailing after, he never allowed one single thread of uncertainty to cross his mind.

"She cannot win, my love. She will die. She must. And we will rule together, as we ought."

"But what if we have miscalculated some tiny point? Suppose she does not react as we plan? What if she proves stronger than we are? What are we to do then?" He takes a ragged breath, and his hand clasps more tightly on hers. "Catherine, I'm afraid."

It takes every bit of her will power not to snatch her hand away, not to strike the head from his shoulders with one swing.

Afraid?! Brin Lütken, afraid of anything in all the galaxies of infinite space?

She closes her eyes, stills her breathing. Taking the chair's controls, she moves him out of the room toward their personal suite. On the way she passes by a well-remembered table and palms a small case without him noticing.

"Come, Brin. Maj Thovold will be here soon, and we want to look our best for her." She takes the tone that one uses to a dimwitted child. "I will help you with your makeup." Her hands shake, and the cosmetic case falls from her palm to the back of the chair. It perches just above his shoulder; he doesn't look back.

Catherine stands up straighter, ceases her trembling, and retrieves the case. Some jobs cannot be delegated. Brin would thank her.

It will be quick. And yet…the twitching death-throes of the thing in the chair will serve as eloquent memorial for the husband she once knew.

The door snaps open, and she wheels him into their dressing room.

XV.
"You come back face to face with us"
Tarantula Nebula, Large Magellanic Cloud
Thursday, 15 April TE 219

Maj almost wishes she hadn't brought the Imperial Eagle. Oh, the crew is not that bad; most of them have served with her in other ships, and Commodore Levenkron is the closest thing she has in the whole Empire to a personal friend. She knows them all by name, from Levenkron down to Spacer First Class Ng Kam See, the most junior of the enlisted personnel assigned to Entertainment & Personal Services. Most of the crew are comfortable with her, and the Bridge crew at least always addresses her as "Supreme Admiral" rather than "Empress."

No, the crew isn't bad. It's the Imperial Retinue that bothers her. Her shipboard Secretary, an unabashed spy who reports regularly to the Imperial Council; a Chief of Protocol whose job consists mainly of telling Maj why she can't do what she wishes; the Press Liaison and her accompaniment of twenty autoservants with holo cameras; the Imperial Physician, whom she has never known to do any work other than watching medical autos and servs and cybs perform their own magic; Ship's Telepath Ensign Liseta Mersand, living proof of the old saw about telepaths and intellectual ability. The best member of the group is Imperial Witness Nav Burgos, eidetic-trained by the Wakmarrel School and fully qualified to give expert testimony before Imperial High Court or Council—and the only reason Nav is so pleasant is that he very rarely speaks.

On the Bridge Maj sits in her special observer's chair and sighs audibly. "Yes, your Majesty?" the Secretary asks.

"Nothing. Leave me alone." She should have made them stay home. Bad enough to drag the enlisted personnel into this —why bring civilians along on what is bound to be the greatest battle of her career? Oh, they ought to be in no danger —but suppose she's miscalculated? Suppose Catherine and

Brin are stronger than she, more devious, more subtle? The officers have all faced death with her before, they are all sworn to do their duty to the Empire. Civilians are quite another matter.

She forces a wry smile. With this particular batch of civilians, what matter if they were killed?

Maybe she ought to have brought the whole Imperial Council along....

"Tarantula Nebula coming up," the pilot reports. On the forward viewscreen, comp-enhanced pictures from the tachyscope show the Nebula as a broadening patch of light that swells in seconds until it encompasses the ship. The pilot's hands fly over her board; Imperial Eagle's velocity drops smoothly.

The fine structure of the Web is too small to see at this speed. Maj turns her attention to a number of data screens before her. There, ship's comp abstracts stills from the tachyscope's view and enhances them to show the Web as a tracery of dark lines. From those stills, the navicomp is able to determine the ship's position.

Out here on the periphery of the Web, things are thin. Here Nebula-stuff still waits to be captured by strands and synthesized into more Web. For a second, Maj has the image of a microbe cruising along the fine hairs on a Human arm, before catching its breath and diving into the skin.

Slowly the Web grows more dense. One screen shifts to a scaled-down holoplot of the entire Web; it shows the ship closing with Imperial Headquarters at ever-decreasing speed. This trip is going to be hard on the Eagle's antigravs; Maj cranes her neck and glances at the Commodore's displays, and is relieved to see that the strain gauges have not yet touched their danger points.

"Final approach coming up, Ma'am."

"Take us in, Commodore."

Suddenly the Web surrounds them (has the microbe reached some inner body cavity?) and Imperial Headquarters floats before them. Imperial Eagle drops out of tachyon phase at precisely the right nanosecond; engines surge, and the Eagle sweeps into a waiting docking bay.

Well, Ancestor, here we are. Now what are we going to do about it?

The Comm Officer turns to Maj. "Message from Sayyid Paula Adelhardt, Ma'am. She gives her compliments and requests that you board the station."

"I'd rather not. Message back to Sayyid Paula: The Empress desires her presence on board the Imperial Eagle. It is also commanded that Tsung-Dao Wu accompany her." Maj bows to the Commodore. "I know that the crew wants to disembark, Richard, but I'm going to have to hold them on the ship. We are effectively in enemy territory, and I'll expect this vessel to be run accordingly."

"Da, Madam."

"I want drones sent out to keep an eye on the surroundings. Full display on the main viewscreen, auxiliary displays in my cabin and the library. Program ship's comp for lookout; tell it to sound an alarm as soon as it picks up any nonstandard movement of the Web."

"Da."

"I shall receive Sayyid Paula and Tsung-Dao in the library. Don't hesitate to disturb me if there are any developments."

"Yes, Ma'am."

"You have the Bridge, Commodore."

Maj is in the library a full ten minutes before anyone arrives. Surrounded by shelf after shelf of datablocks and bookscreens, she stares at display screens and ignores the autoservants who wait patiently for her commands. All right, Catherine and Brin, I'm here. Do your worst.

The door snaps open.

Paula Adelhardt wears green coveralls with the Adelhardt Seal prominently displayed over her substantial breasts. A medium-length cape in pale coral completes her outfit. All in all, she is little changed from the last time Maj saw her. Drop her into the Imperial Council, or any of the interminable dinners and balls held by the Idara, and she would be lost in an instant.

She bows and kisses Maj's hand, and Maj catches first sight of her companion.

The dark hair is greying, the face hardened, and he holds himself like a proud wild beast—but in essence he is the same Sayyid Tsung-Dao Wu who stood before the High Court to hear sentence passed against him. Tarantula, if anything, has agreed with Tsung-Dao; looking into his face Maj almost dares to hope.

He nods his head but does not bow. Maj doesn't offer her hand—if the Chief of Protocol is watching, as he probably is, Maj hopes he will choke.

"Sayyid Adelhardt, Citizen Wu, thank you for coming so quickly."

"Thank you, your Majesty."

Maj cocks her head. "Paula, we don't really have time for that." She glances at the viewscreen—the Web outside is implacable, unchanged. Below the tiny screen, the computer counts off seconds and minutes, spending part of its surplus time in relativistic calculations to keep shipboard time consistent with the Imperial time-tick. Seconds are flicking by too fast.

She looks up, catches a twinkle in Tsung-Dao's eye.

"Citizen Wu, you have the most information to give me. What can you tell me about the plan of our adversaries?"

He settles into a chair. "I assume you're going to want to go after them?"

"Da." No time wasted. He's good, he is.

"They have a fleet of five hundred warships of assorted classes, and some two hundred thousand troops to draw upon from here in the Web. I don't know what sort of support they have back in the Empire."

"If Terrad is telling the truth, they have quite a bit. I'm not concerned with their plan to conquer the Empire—that's obvious and I've done my best to counter any moves they make in that direction. Right now I'm far more interested in their position here. Tsung-Dao, how do I find them?"

He shrugs. "I could take you to their Headquarters. I doubt they'll be there. Listen, Admiral Thovold, you don't realize how much this Web is under their control. Virtually all the settlements of Tarantula are directly allied with them. They have spies all over—I could name you sixteen right off who are here in Imperial Headquarters."

Maj leans forward and steeples her fingers with a tiny smile. "Ah, but you've missed one point. Right now we aren't in Imperial Headquarters. We're in my flagship, and I am—" she touches a stud on her belt "—completely certain that we're secured from observation. Paula, I know I can trust you." You're too stupid to betray me. "Tsung-Dao, I'm going to have to trust you. It doesn't matter, you won't be out of my sight long enough to turn me in."

"Suppose they have a strong telepath keeping watch on me? Suppose they put implants in my inner ears to transmit everything I hear? They might easily have done something like that even without my knowledge."

"That's a chance I must take. Call it a calculated risk."

Their eyes meet, and he abruptly leans back in his chair and grins. "It doesn't matter, does it? You probably want Brin and Catherine to hear your plans, and you're pretending to be careless."

"Or possibly I've had you thoroughly checked over and I know you're not bugging me. Take this line of reasoning as far as you wish, Tsung-Dao. Then be certain of one thing: I've taken it a step further than Brin and Catherine can." She makes an impatient gesture. "None of this matters. For my own reasons, I am trusting you. You two, and no more. Now listen closely: this is what I plan to do now...."

XVI.
"Nets caught the pike, pikes tore the net"
Tarantula Nebula, Large Magellanic Cloud
Thursday, 15 April TE 219

Who is this woman? Tsung-Dao knew Maj Thovold, heard her speak to the Imperial Council, suffered through a long interview with her after his conviction. This is not Maj Thovold.

The Empress he knew was implacable, humorless, a ruthless commander risen from the worst ranks of the Navy and eager to apply military discipline to civilian problems. That earlier Maj would come into the Tarantula Nebula with an entire wing of the Imperial Navy, and would deserve the defeat she took from Masayyid Brin and Catherine.

Who is this stranger? Who is this woman who arrives in a single ship and talks of subtle strategies? What mind animates this body, causes it to behave with a calm surety so unlike the divinely-indifferent commanding presence of the one-time Admiral-who-became-an-Empress?

Looking at her, seeing both weariness and determination burning in her eyes, Tsung-Dao can almost believe that this is a woman who could face Catherine and Brin, and stand a chance of defeating them.

Maybe thirty years of absolute power taught Maj Thovold something. It's possible, isn't it? Tsung-Dao knows how much he learned from his own rule here in the Web—doesn't it stand to reason that a Galaxy would teach more?

Damn, why couldn't she be unlikeable? Why couldn't she behave like the enemy she's been all these years? It just isn't fair! How is a man to know where he stands, if the sides keep changing?

Tsung-Dao doesn't hear the orders Maj gives to her Commodore—they are sealed and secured in the computer already, needing only a flick of her finger to transmit. He follows a step behind as the Empress, along with two Marine

Captains, leads the way to Imperial Eagle's main airlock. The Imperial Retinue, a group of rather silly and pointless people (Tsung-Dao recognizes the type from his own experience) trails along with the Chief of Protocol protesting that it is not wise to leave the flagship's protection, and in any case it is simply unthinkable for her to disembark without proper ceremony.

Maj pointedly pays no attention whatever. Her eyes remain firmly fixed on a datascreen held in the grip of a small autoservant that floats a permanent meter-and-a-half before her. The screen shows an image from remote pickups outside Headquarters: the surrounding Web, dark as usual against white nebular gas.

"I hope she knows what she's doing," Tsung-Dao whispers to Paula.

"She does." Blind faith. Would it be easier, Tsung-Dao wonders, if he could have that sort of blind faith?

It would demn well be easier if he had his blind hatred back.

The main airlock is large enough to hold a company of troops; Tsung-Dao feels lost in it. There is a brief change of air pressure, then the outer door lifts to reveal the docking bay of Imperial Headquarters. "Her Imperial Highness, Empress of the Terran Empire, Protector of Peace, of the Most Supreme Idara of Thovold, Maj." Maj pats her autoservant; she told Tsung-Dao that she'd programmed it to use the most concise possible list of her titles. The full recitation, she said, took over an hour.

A crowd waits. Most of the personnel of Headquarters are gathered just outside the Imperial Eagle; as soon as Maj steps out they break into wild cheering.

She raises her hands; they quiet. Sheep, Tsung-Dao thinks. But is that her fault, or theirs? "Thank you. It's good to be here, good to see you all. I bring you blessings from Terra." She glances at the datascreen. "Now if you will all excuse me, I don't want to disrupt your schedules any longer. Would everyone please return to your regular positions?"

"Your Highness!" a voice from the crowd shouts.

Tsung-Dao is close enough to hear Maj's sigh. "Yes, Citizen?"

A small dark woman in Civil Service uniform pushes her way forward. "Highness, is it true that you're here to save us all from Brin Lütken and Catherine Leonov? Is it true that you're going to keep the Web from going crazy and attacking us?"

"I can see that rumors have been running rampant," Maj says in a half-amused tone. "Sayyid, let me assure you that I am not going to allow any harm to come to this station or to its crew."

The woman bows. "Thank you, your Highness."

"Paula, will you lead?"

On through the station. Tsung-Dao's hand strays on its own accord toward the laser knife dangling at his belt. With a conscious effort, he forces it back.

After a time they reach Paula's salon, the High Imperial style room in which Paula and Tsung-Dao have shared dinners and conversation. Maj gestures, and her party takes seats around the table. She keeps her eyes on the autoservant with the datascreen.

The Chief of Protocol is the first to break the uncomfortable silence. "Begging your pardon, your Highness, but I don"t understand what we're doing here. First you board an Imperial Station without proper ceremony, then you cut short an interview with your subjects, and now—"

The look on Maj's face is one that Tsung-Dao vows to learn. "Ever since we entered this galaxy we have been in a state of war. Right now I'm simply waiting for the shoe to drop." She reaches to her belt and removes her mobile, sets it on the table before her. "Maj Thovold to Imperial Eagle. Commodore Levenkron, unseal your orders now and execute them without delay."

"Your servant, Admiral."

Maj holds up a hand, points to the datascreen. "Watch."

For a few seconds nothing happens; then the view rotates slightly to include Imperial Headquarters. The Imperial Eagle slowly drifts out of the docking bay.

"Eagle to Empress. As per orders, we are withdrawing to make contact with the rest of the Fleet."

The Imperial Secretary is on his feet. "Empress, I must protest this unwise—"

"Quiet." The Eagle accelerates, then fades into tachyon phase. Before afterimages can fade, the flagship is gone.

Tsung-Dao fixes his eyes intently upon Maj. She looks back at him with a raised eyebrow. Wait, her face tells him. Wait and see.

On the datascreen the Web is space-black against curling white clouds. Then, so quickly that Tsung-Dao thinks he might have imagined it, a flash of electric blue lights one strand, then another. In a few heartbeats, it is as if lightning is zapping across the Web.

Paula looks at her own personal datapad and frowns. "The Web is moving, your Highness. Closing up. Coming closer."

Maj nods. "Sound your alarms. Prepare this station for evacuation." Her gaze sweeps around the table. "Not us."

In the background, sirens wail. Tsung-Dao just hopes that Imperial personnel are well-trained in evacuation drill.

The station, up until now steady in its artificial grav, shifts ever so slightly. On the screen Tsung-Dao sees a kilometers-long Web strand slap the station hard.

"Your Highness—"

"I thought I asked for quiet."

"But Majesty—"

"Is that quiet? When I give an order, I expect it to be obeyed." She turns to Paula and Tsung-Dao. "I'm sorry, apparently the children have been up past their bedtime." She waves at the screen, where more strands are converging on the station. "Is this what happened to you two?"

"Da."

"Good. We've established that they can control this portion of the Web."

Paula taps her datapad. "All personnel are in lifeboats and away. Except us."

The room lurches, this time more violently. Maj Thovold remains seated at the head of the table, her face calm. Even

Tsung-Dao is a bit worried—has she miscalculated? Is she too confident?

The strongest lurch yet nearly topples Tsung-Dao from his seat. All lights go off, and grav drops to nothing. The only illumination left is the steady glow from Maj's datascreen.

Screams, flying bodies, total pandemonium—and in the midst of it all sits a straight-backed woman in Imperial Navy uniform, her arms folded, her face impassive. What, Tsung-Dao wonders, is she made of?

Appearing on the viewscreen as if from nowhere, a great black eagle-shape swoops down upon the station, snapping Web strands that attempt to take hold of it. Maj Thovold smiles as the salon's hull buckles, and a starboat belches six Imperial Marines with vacuum gear ready. Tsung-Dao closes his own vacuum helmet; at the same time the Empress tightens the hood of a uniform that also serves as a vacuum suit.

In less than twenty seconds all are aboard the boat and the station is falling behind. Minutes later they are back on board the flagship. "Highness, that was a fantastic display of courage and—"

"Save it for the press. Our job isn't over." The Eagle's Executive Officer is standing by as soon as the boat's hatch opens.

"Supreme Admiral, your orders have been followed. All lifeboats are recovered and all station personnel accounted for. Fusion bombs have been set. In one hundred sixty seconds we will withdraw to one-half lightyear. The bombs will detonate in two hundred seconds."

"Good. Escort these people to their cabins. Paula and Tsung-Dao, come with me to the Bridge."

The autoservant still loyally clutches its datascreen; Tsung-Dao glances at it and can't help a gasp. All eyes turn to the image.

On Webstuff against Nebula, outlined in violet and deepest ozone blue, is a picture of a face he knows well.

Catherine Leonov. Laughing.

Maj shakes her head. "Bridge. Now."

XVII.
"Steaming drift and dust"
Tarantula Nebula, Large Magellanic Cloud
Thursday, 15 April TE 219

Hours later, Paula still can't stop shaking. Horrible, horrible. Just like that other time, with Tsung-Dao, when the Web collapsed upon her—only this time worse, much worse. She saw the wreckage of Imperial Headquarters, saw the cleansing light of fusion bombs before drones overloaded and failed. And that terrible image, that face drawn across the sky. For tenday upon tenday she lived surrounded by the Web, totally ignorant of its baleful scrutiny, ignorant of the power that lived just under those strands and nodes, ignorant of the mind that waited beyond it all....

Now she sits in an observer's chair on the Bridge and watches the Empress. Trying to draw some kind of courage from the sight of her leader. If anyone can instill courage in her, it is Maj Thovold.

Can anyone ever make Paula brave again?

The Commodore had bad news. "Admiral, the Web is in motion all about us. Strands are readjusting themselves to shut off charted escape paths. Concentrations of dust block other routes. There are planetoids astray in there. Every Wolf-Rayet star in this sector seems to have cut loose with massive flares. If we move now, we may be able to get out with half our antigravs. A few hours from now, we may not even have that much of a chance."

Tsung-Dao has been quiet up until now—thinking, or perhaps as frightened as Paula is herself. Now he bows his head before the Empress. "Sayyid, I'm concerned about my people. With all this disturbance in the Web they may get hurt."

"Clanna Wu, I honestly do not think your people are in danger—at least, no more danger than they live with each day. Brin and Catherine need them to crew their ships, nyet?"

"Who knows what they'll do? The lives of bystanders mean nothing to them…they've made that clear. You're safe; you've demonstrated that you can stand against the worst they throw. But my people…"

"Surely you don't think that was the worst Catherine Leonov and Brin Lütken can do?" The Empress leans forward in her chair; Paula hugs her arms tightly about herself. "That was a love-tap. A formal declaration of war, and nothing else. No one, least of all Brin and Catherine, ever thought I would fall in that assault."

"And what happens now?" Paula hates to ask, hates to know that there is an answer. She wants to go back to the Empire, back to the Idara's estates on Dunsinane and townhouses on Leikeis and the hunting preserve on Taiphan. She wants to give up all this fear and pain and go back to a world she knew and loved, a world where she was secure.

"The next move is mine. Tsung-Dao, you've reminded me that we have people in potential danger here. Minor readjustments in the structure of the Web are not going to harm any of its inhabitants—but you're right, we don't know what Catherine and Brin will try next. So…we take the offensive to them."

Paula can't stop a moan from escaping her throat. No one seems to notice.

The Commodore frowns. "Highness, I remind you that we have civilians aboard. The personnel from the Imperial Headquarters. Your Retinue."

"My Retinue is pledged to follow me anywhere; now we'll have a chance to test their oaths. As for the civilians—condemn it, you're right. Just like Brin and Catherine to saddle me with them. Comm—do you have contact with any Imperial ships from Headquarters?"

"All of them, Ma'am."

"Have them rendezvous to pick up base personnel. Then tell them to shape for the Empire along the fastest orbits."

"Ma'am, the condition of the Web—"

"All right. What sort of pilots are aboard those ships?"

The Info/Comp Officer has the answer ready. "None with a piloting rating above seven."

Paula, whose own rating is barely a three, was always impressed by the Headquarters pilots. In an environment like this, though, with loose masses flying about and the Web providing parsecs of sold obstacles, she didn't think most of them had a chance to get out safely.

Apparently Maj thinks so too. She frowns, then looks up with her command face on. "Our relief pilots are both fourteens, aren't they?"

"Da."

"Good. Rendezvous those ships, pick the best two, and cram all their personnel into those two, and send them home with our pilots." She casts a glance at the pilot on the Eagle's helm. "How about it, Commander Spiwak? Can you handle Imperial Eagle by yourself?"

"Been flying this pretty bird for twenty years, Admiral. Imagine I can keep it up for a while longer."

"Good. Carry out the operation and be prepared for departure in fifteen minutes. Tsung-Dao, Paula, come with me. We have a course to plot. Navigator, hand your station over to your relief and come with us. Commodore, we'll be in the tactics room. You have the Bridge."

Paula forces her dry throat to make intelligible sounds. "Your Highness, where are we going next?"

The Empress gestures at the forward viewscreen, where the Web moves like seaweed at the change of tides. "Brin and Catherine have given us an invitation; it would be rude to refuse. Tsung-Dao, you know where we're headed."

"To Them."

"Correct. You know the way?"

"I feel sure," Tsung-Dao says slowly, "That I was allowed to know the way for just this eventuality."

"Probably so. Probably so." Maj looks about, then claps her hands. "Step lively, Citizens. We have a war to fight."

XVIII.
"Hell's iron gin"
Tarantula Nebula, Large Magellanic Cloud
Thursday, 15 April TE 219

Deeper into the Web. Maj keeps her eyes on the viewscreen; but really she sees nothing. Her mind idlws, relaxed yet busy. All plans are made, all contingencies prepared for, all loopholes (she hopes) patched.

And the Web races past. Pilot brings the ship out of tachyon phase, makes a careful vector change, drops them back into faster-than-light for an instant, and repeats. The journey is an endless succession of hop-skip-jump, and all the time praying to whatever gods there are that fragile antigravs hold together. Already one antigrav has blown—Maintenance works furiously to replace it. There are only a few more spares.

Well, Ancestor, this is the telling trip. You've faced your dangers, now I face mine. Are we any different? You on a storm-lashed ocean many sleeps from any land; me in twisted and knotted space days from my Galaxy and my people. Gods above, whatever brought us to this extreme?

It is our nature, the ghost answers her.

To fight. And the outcome? That is up to the shades of ancestors and the unknown forces that shape destiny.

Nonsense. She is thinking like an old woman. Superstition. The battle is decided by the strengths of those involved. On the one hand, Maj Thovold: fighter, leader, thinker, doer. On the other, Brin Lütken and Catherine Leonov: schemers, dictators, cunning but too impatient. The contest will decide itself.

Out of tachyon phase. "Antigrav Six has blown, Ma'am. Five is coming back on-line in just a few seconds."

Maj sighs. "Put a mech crew on Six and get it repaired. How many spares after that?"

"Two."

The Commodore says nothing else. He doesn't need to; Maj has eyes, she can read strain gauges as well as anyone else.

"When the next one blows, have it replaced but don't bring it on-line. We'll operate with one antigrav down for the duration of this flight."

"Yes, Ma'am."

The Imperial Eagle is a well-designed, superbly-balanced ship. She can, if need be, fly in clear space with only three of her six antigravs operating. This is not, however, clear space; and the same tachyon vesicles that drive her antigravs also give her faster-than-light tachyon phase capability and defense screens.

Without those, the Eagle is a grounded bird without defense. "ETA to destination?"

"Twenty-seven minutes with one antigrav down. Add another fifteen if we have to fly with two down."

"And with three down?"

"Grav interference gets worse the closer we get to destination. There are planetoid-sized masses swinging around in complex patterns there."

"How much longer with only three antigravs?"

"With all due respect, Ma'am, I'm a Pilot, not a miracle worker."

So. Two spares will have to do. "Physician…get the Telepath up here. Give her her drugs and hypnotize her, and get her in contact with Fleet Headquarters. Just in case. And make sure she stays near me."

"Admiral, Antigrav Number Three just blew."

Demn.

It seems to Maj that the Eagle crawls those last lighthours centimeter by centimeter. Worse than her first campaigns at the tail end of the Formation Wars, worse than the longest Imperial Council session on record. At last the flagship bursts into a huge cavity of solid Webstuff, and Maj sees the gleam of dellsite metal glinting in the powerful searchlights, just the way Tsung-Dao described it.

"Pilot, dock with that station." Maj kept herself alert—surely Catherine and Brin will not allow them to walk right in….

The computer catches the attack before any of them; alarms are sounding before Maj even knows what to look for. Without electric flashes, without looming faces, without any fuss at all, the Web cavity is collapsing on them, at the same time sprouting tendrils that reach eagerly for the ship.

Pilot's eyes are wild. "Ma'am, we've got incredible strains. Asteroidal masses moving everywhere within half a lightyear. They must've been preparing for this for years. Strains are going off the board."

Now the computer sounds a new and different alarm. Instrument boards already tell the story, as does the sudden loss of cabin gravity: Imperial Eagle is without antigravs, without tachyon converter, without defense screens.

Without hope.

Never that. Maj leans back in her chair and buckles her safety straps. "Commodore, give them our response. Polarizers on all screens."

Lights race across the boards, current is diverted, laser dispersions set to their maximum, mirrors deploy—and the Imperial Eagle all at once shines with the light of suns, a white light that would blaze bright against the largest solar flare.

The advancing Web stops, then it actually retreats.

"Wha...?" Tsung-Dao's mouth hangs open.

Maj grins. "The Web gets its energy from star- and Nebula-light. That's why our biotechs designed it black. Whatever else she altered, Catherine couldn't change that without us noticing. Give it enough light, and it gives the phototropic response: spread maximum surface and absorb."

"She'll figure a way around that."

"I imagine so. But we still have one spare antigrav, and once we get it hooked up we can shift to tachyon phase. If our present low velocity goes reciprocal-light we'll be kiloparsecs away by the time the engines realize they've blown."

The Ship Systems Officer's eyes have been firmly attached to her data screens; now she lifts her head and turns a look of horror on the Empress. "Highness...our remaining spare antigrav has been sabotaged. The tachyon vesicle is useless."

XIX.
"Still sweet and keen"
Tarantula Nebula, Large Magellanic Cloud
Thursday, 15 April TE 219

Brin is not happy. Catherine stands beside his chair, her hands resting lightly on his arm. Cold his body is, cold and stiff. Death-mask makes of his face a twisted pouting frown. His eyes stare slightly left of forward. No matter, one spouse knows what the other is feeling.

"You must not be upset, Brin. We thought she would have some way to escape from this trap."

Brin's stare reproaches her.

"So I do not push the offensive. Do you think I could not, if I wanted? I could easily tighten the Web in defiance of the phototropic response."

Then why not, Brin's eyes seem to question.

"Her ship is without engines. We still have asteroids running interference. Our personal star yacht is the only vessel around for parsecs, and Tsung-Dao knows this. If Maj Thovold wants to get home, she will have to come through here." Catherine hugs the stiff shoulders, plants a kiss on the cold forehead. "And I am waiting for her, love. I am waiting."

Brin says nothing, merely stares slightly to the left of forward.

XX.
"Since first the Devil threw dice with God"
Tarantula Nebula, Large Magellanic Cloud
Thursday, 15 April TE 219

"You can't!"

Tsung-Dao pounds his fist against the arm of his chair. "Maj, you just can't. They're going to be in there waiting for you. You'll be marching into Their territory, and taking the rest of us with you."

The Empress' smile does not falter. "Tsung-Dao, you must learn to trust me. Right now we have no other escape. Oh, I could have Telepath summon rescue ships from Fleet Headquarters, and we would all say farewell to the Web—after they take a day and a half to get here. That's not what I came here for, and you know it. Catherine and Brin have challenged me, and now they're waiting at the appointed place of combat. What choice have I but to keep my appointment?"

"You don't have to make it sound like some kind of epic battle."

She cocks her head. "Isn't it, though? Don't you think they'll remember this fight for years? That's one of the great things about being Empress…everything I do gets remembered." She looks a bit wistful. "Maybe that's enough."

"I think it's suicide."

"It is suicide for an untrained civilian to go into battle with unfamiliar weapons. For a soldier with her accustomed arms, it's a day's work. There's a difference. This is a day's work." She shakes her head. "You're sure that their personal yacht is beyond that station?"

"They keep it on the other side of the Web, docked with their Headquarters. Catherine made sure I knew where it was. I can't guarantee that it'll be there now."

"Fair enough." She calls the Commodore over. "Three of our gigs will hold all the crew and the assorted hangers-on." She looks pointedly at her Retinue. "Let's board those gigs and get going."

"Boarding order?"

"In my gig I want the Retinue, Paula, Tsung-Dao, our Pilot, Telepath, yourself, and Marines to round out the balance. Divide up the others as it suits you. The other two gigs are to remain ready for launch until they receive further orders—or until ten hours pass without hearing from any of us. Then command passes down along the standard chain until there are no survivors. I don't expect that last to become necessary. Please tell the crew I said so."

"Highness?" Maj's Secretary raises a tentative hand. Tsung-Dao wrinkles his nose—how can a woman like Maj have chosen such an insipid nobody as her personal Secretary?

"Da?"

"In case—now of course we don't expect it—but just in case something goes wrong…Highness, you have not yet designated your successor. I think we ought to be able to carry word of your choice back to the Empire."

"Oh, do you? All right, I can see the justice of your request. Witness, make sure you're getting this. Telepath, transmit to Fleet Headquarters." The Empress takes a breath, catches Tsung-Dao's eye, and gives him a watch-this expression. "In case I am killed in this upcoming battle, I make the same choice of successor that Alexander did."

"Eh?"

"Let the Empire go to the strongest." Maj laughs.

The Secretary stamps his foot, bounding off the deck in zero-grav. "Highness, this is no time for jokes."

"What makes you think I'm joking?"

"Highness, such an action would throw the Empire into civil war. Everything we've worked for could be toppled."

"Then you'd better hope I win, hadn't you?" She looks the Secretary straight in the eye. "If I die, that means Brin and Catherine win. And their next target will be the Empire. Don't you want the strongest person in charge?" She ignores the Secretary's fuming expression and slaps the Commodore across the back. "We've wasted too much time. Richard, let's get on with this."

Tsung-Dao follows Maj to the gig, his head low. To the strongest…well, if she dies, Catherine and Brin would be the strongest. At least the Empire gave the Web benign neglect and the ability to build its own societies—Catherine and Brin took total command of it, and now the very structure of his people's homes can be made to attack them.

Tsung-Dao doesn't know the names of very many gods; and those he knows are from the home Galaxy. They have never answered his prayers, way out here in the Greater Cloud. Just the same, he quickly mouths a prayer to all of them: Let her win.

XXI.
"So rang, thrown down, the devil's die"
Tarantula Nebula, Large Magellanic Cloud
Thursday, 15 April TE 219

If only, Paula thinks, a lifeboat's antigravs were strong enough to serve in the Imperial Eagle's engines. But one might just as well ask a hundred-watt bulb to light a city. Maj Thovold is right—there is no way out and no way home but through Brin and Catherine's lair, and Paula just had to get used to the idea.

All the same, memory of a sinister face burned across the sky disturbs her. She has no desire to meet the owner of that face, the controller of all that power.

The gig holds thirty. Paula straps herself into a seat next to a group of Imperial Marines; their space-black uniforms and battle-gear give her scant comfort.

No help for it now. All she can do was bite her lip and follow Maj wherever the Empress leads. And if she had to die, well, she would do it as a member of Idara Adelhardt, and be damned if any of these Marines would see her giving up her responsibility. With the exception of Maj—and Tsung-Dao, whose status is questionable—Paula is the only representative of the Idara aboard this gig. The voices of her teachers and generations of breeding remind her that she has an obligation to fulfill.

This is what being Idara is all about, Paula thinks. It gives us a reason to go on, when all we want to do is crawl into a corner and hide.

The gig is off.

It's a short trip, less than a kilometer. Docking bays are open; they respond to the autopilot's commands and soon the gig is safely secured.

Safely?

Maj stands, looks back at the crew. "Citizens, friends… thank you for coming this far with me. We have a little further to go, and then we'll be free. I hope. Will you come with me?"

Paula closes her eyes. Her responsibility. She stands, then kneels to the Empress. "For the Empire."

"To the glory of the Empire!" Nineteen Marines fall to their knees, laser rifles offered in homage. Commodore and Pilot kneel, bow their heads. The Imperial Retinue goes down, all but the Witness and the slack-jawed Telepath.

With surprise, Paula watches Tsung-Dao lower himself to the floor. "For the Empire," he whispers.

Maj nods. "Let's go."

The gig's airlock opens—and the air is full of tiny flying things. Insects? No. Microbots, each less than a centimeter across, each trailing loops of strong cord. They dive and swoop, and it is at once apparent that their intention is to bind the crew.

The Marines respond at once, firing with computer perfection, setting up portable defense screens, countering this attack with a concerted effort that they make look as easy as turning over in bed.

One of the microbots dives at a Marine, thumps against and through her chest. There is the sound of a muffled explosion, and the Marine slumps deckward with blood wetting her uniform.

"Hold fire!" Maj commands. "Let them take us. No sense in dying here one at a time."

No sense at all, Paula agrees, pulling her eyes away from the bloody form on the deck.

But where, she wonders as microbots bind her, where will we die?

They are dragged through long corridors at a forced march. Maj keeps her head high; Paula sees her exchange whispered comments with the Major General who commands these Marines, but she can't hear what they say.

They enter a large empty room, a room whose walls are holoscreens looking out on various sections of the Web. Autoservants come upon them, larger ones with many waldoes. In minutes the entire company is stripped, all weapons and other instruments taken away. Paula swallows hard and fights tears—she keeps her eyes on Maj Thovold's proud face, and tries to remember her duty to the people about her. All the while little voices in her mind scream at her, berate her for trusting the Empress. No matter how proud, how competent Maj Thovold looks, she is nothing but an old woman facing death. All her subtlety, all her plans and counterplans—what has happened to them now?

Paula cannot answer.

Finally they are left alone, a pitiful group huddled together under the brooding presence of the Web. It is not even necessary to keep them bound—a ring of autoservants around the perimeter of the room keeps lasers trained on each and every member of the group.

"I suppose," Maj says in a casual voice, "you're all wondering why I've asked you here yoday." The ancient joke receives no laughter.

"Greetings, Maj Thovold." Against the background of the Web, two forms appear. One is seated in a wheelchair—the other stands behind it, pushing the chair forward. As they draw closer, Paula recognizes the face of the seated man from history holos: Brin Lütken. But he is twisted so unnaturally, his face grimaced…dead. Doesn't the other know?

The other figure looks up, and Paula sees the face that burned across the Web, the face of Catherine Leonov. She shivers. There is the memory of beauty on that face, but it is long gone—just as life is long gone from the body of Brin Lütken. Wrinkled, pale, Catherine's face is a distorted reflection of Maj Thovold's. The eyes are the deep blue of Terra's oceans; they at least are still alive and alert. They touch upon Paula, and seem to gaze into her mind for an instant before dismissing her casually.

"You are not in a very good tactical position, Empress, are you?"

"You think not?" Paula has the feeling that Maj has forgotten her, forgotten the rest of her companions—that Maj and Catherine Leonov are on their own astral plane, that battle is begun, and Maj has no time to spare for other thoughts.

"Seems so. Those Marines are not going to help you, your Highness." Catherine sneers the title, making it an insult.

"I don't expect them to."

"You are not going to ask me for their lives?"

"Their lives aren't yours to give."

"As that may be. Step forward, Maj Thovold, so my autos can have a clear shot at you. No sense in getting your playmates killed in the bargain. I may have use for them later."

"No doubt." Maj takes a single step forward.

"A little closer than that, if you will. I want to see you die myself. Brin wants to see it."

Catherine turns the chair slightly. Maj advances another step. "I don't think Brin is in much condition to see anything right now." Another step. Paula sees the Major General tensing.

"Please explain to your followers that if they attempt to interfere, they will die instantly."

Without taking her eyes off Catherine, Maj makes a motion with her right hand. The Major General closes his eyes, lets out breath, and clenches his fists in helplessness.

"Would you rather have a countdown, Highness, or should I surprise you?"

"Whatever you please." Maj is now only ten meters from Catherine; she takes another step forward.

"Enough. Stay there."

"Why? Are you afraid?" Step. "I thought you wanted to see my agony up close." Step.

"My eyesight is fine. Stop there."

Maj takes another step.

Catherine raises her hand. "Fire at my signal."

Paula seethes with frustration. Her Empress…her sworn leader…is about to be executed by a woman no better than a thug. Well, if no one else will act—she will show them of what stuff a daughter of Idara Adelhardt is made!

"For the Empire!" She jumps forward, intending to shield the body of the Empress with her own. Autos are far too quick;

pain lances along her side and she falls, rolls, pulls herself up. Why is she still alive?

Catherine ignores her. Before Paula can do anything else, the woman drops her hand and ten lines of ruby light draw themselves in the air between autoservants and the body of the Empress…

…And halt half a meter from Maj Thovold, soaked up by a shimmer of pale red the color of rich blood.

The pain conquers her, and Paula faints.

XXII.
"She loved the games men played with death" Tarantula Nebula, Large Magellanic Cloud Thursday, 15 April TE 219

Maj sighs with relief.

It has been more than a third of a century since she tried her defense implants. She had them installed when she made Rear Admiral; they'd saved more than one shipload of loyal men and women. The autoservants who performed the operations under Terrad's guidance had been wiped of all memory; Maj was careful that no one knew she had defense screens, a functional antigrav, and an assortment of other weapons safely secured inside her body.

Of course, there was a price to pay. Most of her implants are powered by a miniature reactor nestled next to her colon — filtered hydrogen from the water in her blood goes to the reactor while the oxygen is dissolved to make her somewhat independent of breathing gear. But the receptors and transmitters for her screens and other implants make use of her own neural pathways, damaging them as they do so. The devices produce a good deal of waste heat that passes into her bloodstream, and the reactor has only minimal shielding. Even before she became Empress Maj had given up hope of a dynasty—now she had to face the danger of even worse radiation damage.

Ten minutes, Maj thinks. Ten minutes and then unconsciousness, as she is drained of life-force. There is an override circuit she has never dared to use; it would give her perhaps an additional five minutes at full power.

So be it.

She steps forward once more, keeping her eyes fixed on the unbelieving face of Catherine Leonov. Two steps, then three; Catherine raises her hands and the useless laser assault ceases. Maj's sight blurs briefly at the flicker of her defense screen as it radiates all the stored-up energy, then clears to only the usual curtain of summer-haze.

"What's the matter, Catherine?" Maj grins. "Don't you know that the Empress is divine? I'm a goddess."

Catherine leaves her dead husband's side and takes a step in Maj's direction. Now her face twists from astonishment into hate. She raises scarred and wrinkled arms, and a defense screen of her own envelopes her with a shimmer.

"Do you not know, Maj Thovold, that I am a demon?"

They close upon one another.

Defense screens interpenetrate with a flash of fire and a burst of ultrawave static that probably overloads all receivers for lightyears around. Catherine swings an arm; Maj feels her own hands move at lightning speed as her defense computer activates her nerves. Her left arm meets Catherine's blow in a halo of sparks; nails too strong to be anything Human rake her arm and she almost pulls it back.

Her own right arm straightens and, without any conscious thought on her part, thrusts itself deep into Catherine's screen; A laser, firing through Maj's middle fingertip, pumps megawatts into Catherine's defenses. The energy radiates away harmlessly.

Maj sees a kick coming, ducks, and scores a burn on the swinging leg. One minute into battle; she steps back to take stock of herself.

Her left arm, bloodied, hangs limp. Some kind of poison has been injected, no doubt—she hopes the synthesizer buried in her abdomen can cope with it. Her right arm is stiff, but the bones are dellsite-strengthened, nothing could break it short of a fusion blast—and that couldn't penetrate her screen.

Catherine looks calm, poised for another attack. She whispers in another language—"Gankeh ebettor"—a curse? Then, she leaps.

Maj jumps, feels her antigrav surge, and flies to the ceiling. Catherine is ten centimeters behind her. Above the heads of the crew, they meet again.

Fast...the woman is faster than Maj. Two of Catherine's blows connect one after another: one lays bare a long scratch on Maj's back, the other cuts her temple and stops a bare millimeter before her left eye.

There is opportunity, glimpsed and acted upon in picoseconds by the computer; Maj's right hand grips Catherine's left wrist and dellsite clamps lock fingerbones in place. Catherine will not escape this grip. Before Catherine can counterattack, Maj swings up her right foot, lifts her toes, and applies to Catherine's wrist the fine-edged dellsite blade that suddenly sprouts there. She tugs and twists, then all at once she flies across the room, Catherine's detached hand in her own.

One glimpse is enough. The hand is still organic, but rebuilt to a much greater degree than Maj's body. This hand is a miracle of engineering. Before she can stop it, it twists about and catches onto the back of her hand, starts crawling up her arm.

No wonder Catherine is so much faster. If every part of her body is as well-constructed as this hand, she is a virtual android. Maj's augmented nerve impulses travel in excess of a kilometer per second—Catherine's must move at the speed of light.

The hand, at least, is not protected by a defense screen. A miniature laser turret hides under Maj's breastbone, aimed by the direction of her eyesight—Maj looks steadily at the hand and it falls off, smoking, and then explodes.

Catherine attacks again.

It goes on. Attack, counter. Slash and duck, twist and slash again, to have her hand swoop through empty air. And now Catherine is grinning, a death-mask covered with flecks of splattered blood.

Terrad programmed Maj's attack computer. Maj wonders where Catherine gets her reactions from. Is this to be a battle of computers? If so, Maj is sure to lose—the little set of chips fused to her hipbones cannot hope to compete with whatever large mechanisms Catherine uses.

But...radio doesn't penetrate defense screens. So Catherine has to be getting her reactions via ultrawave. Simple. Maj jumps for Catherine, tries a few times before getting a grip on a thrashing ankle, then sets her clamps and holds on.

Interpenetrating defense screens. Ultrawave static. And now they are both on in-body systems, no matter how much brainpower Catherine has waiting outside her skin. Sooner or later Catherine will run out of pre-set attack plans, and then it will be an even match of comps. The battle will be between enemies again.

Nine minutes. Without even thinking, Maj triggers her override system. Enough time to worry about the consequences later.

She sees an opening, moves quickly—and finds that Catherine moves even faster. Maj is in a grip as strong as her own, and Catherine's free arm sprouts a set of manipulators. Sharp metal claws move toward Maj's throat.

Maj's computer grows more daring. She feels a twist in her gut, a searing pain, and then gravity goes all strange around her. When she regains her equilibrium, she and Catherine are frozen like wrestlers, each one's freedom of movement restricted by the other. Long seconds it goes on, eyes staring into eyes.

Faster than a striking viper, Catherine ducks her head and ccmes away with a piece of Maj's shoulder in her teeth. She spits. "You cannot win, Maj Thovold. If there is no other way to kill you, I will cut loose my reactor. Close as you are, your defense screen will not save you from that blast."

"You're…wrong…Catherine. I can…still…do this!" Pain is everywhere—but Terrad has foreseen every contingency and provided her the exact program she needs. It must work — there can be no second try.

Her antigrav goes into wild fibrillations, grav waves sweep the room with mad unpredictability and spread outward through the Nebula. No tachyon vesicle, this close, can possibly resist the strain.

Even before her own antigrav blows out, Maj sees the defense screen glow fade from around Catherine, and she knows that her enemy has lost her essential systems. Now,

now while there is feedback through Catherine's body, now while they are both falling—

Maj thrusts her right hand forward, driven with the full power of inhumanly-strengthened muscles. Catherine's chest offers no resistance, nor do the bodily organs in the way. Maj draws out her hand and plunges again, stirs within living flesh as Catherine's screams ring in her ears.

There are only a few spots in the human torso where a bulky piece of equipment like a reactor could hide. Maj finds Catherine's on the second try. By then it doesn't much matter: her first thrust already severed Catherine's spine, disconnecting the reactor from the brain that controlled it.

One more duty left. With a right arm that hurts beyond all pain—surely those last thrusts pulped all that was human about it—Maj hammers until Catherine's skull splits. Then, with a blast from her chest laser, she reduces the brain within to ashes.

Twenty-three seconds short of complete system overload, Maj switches off her overrides and her body returns to normal.

The Physician is at her side at once, with injections that numb the pain and life-support packages from Brin's chair. Maj is grateful for his help—without it, she might not last through what must come next.

"W-Witness, come forward." Amazing that her vocal cords still work. "Remember what you see and hear. Telepath, transmit to Fleet Headquarters and the Imperial Council." She coughs, pain flares. "Tsung-Dao Wu, I restore your title and your position. I pardon you of all remaining punishment and all crimes against the Empire. Sayyid Tsung-Dao of Idara Wu, step forward." One eye is out of focus; she ignores it. Tsung-Dao approaches, kneels next to her. He is crying.

"Give me your hand." Neither of her arms respond. She lays her head against his hand, and as gently as she can, bites the fleshy part of his thumb until she tastes blood. Her own blood coats both her cheeks; she rubs it into his wound. "There, that'll give you the drop of Imperial Blood you need. We are one blood and one flesh now, Sayyid Tsung-Dao Wu. Here before all witnesses I do proclaim you, Tsung-Dao of the Idara Wu, my heir and successor. All hail Tsung-Dao Wu, Emperor!"

He pulls back. "That's not funny, Maj."

Her Secretary pushes into her visual field. "Highness—"

She rolls her good eye at the Secretary. "For the last time, shut up. Tsung-Dao, if I were you I'd have this one executed for terminal stupidity. Should have done it years ago." She tries to nod her head toward Brin's body. "You can probably get some methods from him."

"Maj, I don't want your Throne."

"Of course you don't. I didn't want it either. Demn it, Tsung-Dao, you're the only one. You're now the most able administrator in two galaxies. Listen, man. I was the fighter, the conqueror. I started out as a heretic and wound up a goddess.

"Tsung-Dao, I made an Empire work. I took two trillion banal, boring, conservative idiots and prevented them from smothering one another in mutual contempt. I took over their minds and emotions, I told them what to think and feel, and I removed every person with enough will and individuality to stand up to me and tell me I was wrong."

She moves her chin in the direction of her huddled crew. "Look at them. Worker ants, they'll follow any Queen who happens along and talks loud enough. Which is why I sent millions to Tarantula and places like it. I needed drones.

"Well, that job's done now. What was once radical is now tradition. The Throne is now the Establishment, and it's strong enough to withstand the presence of men and women of ability. It's been thirty-two of the most boring years known to humanity, and now we're ready for the men and women of ability to come back, ready to let them take charge and face new challenges. I tamed the populace for you, Tsung-Dao. Now it's your job to lead them." It hurts, Ancestor. But I suppose you suffered too, you and your mother and all before you. We are the ones who suffer, aren't we? We are the ones who can stand it.

"I knew you'd all be here when I needed you. Even in the most hostile environment I could devise, you survived. You thrived. It made you stronger. I've been watching you, all this time, and you've done me proud.

"Catherine gravitated here because she thought she could use you and the thousands like you. She was the last challenge I had to face, and now she's out of the way. And you proved that you will never remain corrupted by her like." Maj's head throbs. The room is thick with ghosts, waiting for her to take her place among them.

"Come back, Tsung-Dao. And bring the others with you. The Empire needs you."

"Highness," Chief of Protocol intones, "This is hardly legal and proper."

Maj forces a smile. "See? That's why they need you." Gods, Ancestors, whatever powers are there…I've been so lonely.

Tsung-Dao nods, presses his lips to the marks of her teeth in his hand, then bends and kisses her forehead. "I can hardly refuse. But I won't make the same mistake you did—I won't make it a lifetime job."

"It is, whether you want it or not." Yes, Ancestor, I'm coming. Wait for me, I'll be along in a moment. "Watch out for Chen. They're the most powerful Idara. You'll need to check that power. Terrad knows. You shouldn't have any trouble changing the access codes. The staff will show you how."

For a moment, she feels herself drifting away, as if she is falling asleep. With a start, she pulls herself back. "Tsung-Dao?"

"Da?"

"It is worth it. When you doubt, remember: it is worth it."

"I'll remember."

Rough hands are under her head, and she looks into her Physician's face. "Highness, we have full life-support equipment here. If you can stay awake for just a few more seconds, you'll be safe. We can rebuild you an entire body… clone a new one and transplant your brain."

"No."

"Highness…"

"No. That's an order. Demn, my chance finally comes, the fight is over...and you want to make me stay. Turn those condemned machines off."

"She's not lucid. Witness, please note that I am taking charge as ward until..." The Physician's voice fades to nothing as Tsung-Dao reaches out and very deliberately switches off the medical equipment that is attaching itself to Maj's body.

She tries to smile again. Her eyes seek out Tsung-Dao, and she knows he meets her gaze. "Thank you."

Maj Thovold, at the side of her Ancestor, sets off in search of other oceans to conquer.

Paula Adelhardt, very carefully keeping her eyes from the body on the floor, kneels before Tsung-Dao. "Hail Tsung-Dao Wu, Emperor." She kisses his hand, and stays on her knees.

One by one, the others in the room sink to their knees. "Hail Tsung-Dao Wu, Emperor."

Tsung-Dao turns to Imperial Eagle's Commodore. "Let's see about that starship. Telepath, tell the Empire that we're coming home."

From *Encyclopedia Terranica*, New York, Terra, TE 375:

Thovold, Maj

First Empress of the Terran Empire TE 187-219

b. 24 January TE 123, Geled
d. 15 April TE 219, Tarantula Nebula, Lesser Magellanic Cloud

She was the third of seven children of Alb Thovold and Trinka Stenholz. The family, which had settled on Geled in the late 80s, was poor, and Maj and her siblings were introduced to hard work and strong discipline at an early age.

Maj was a fun-loving youth who enjoyed sports, while taking only a moderate interest in her studies. She passed her adulthood qualifying exams in TE 140, and then entered the Imperial Naval Academy at Zvyozdny Gorodok. She excelled in soccer but injured a knee in her second year and was forced to stop playing. She graduated in the class of TE 145, ranking 488th academically and 998th in discipline out of the total of 1312 graduates.

She was commissioned an Ensign and was sent to Novy Stalingrad. She was assigned to patrol duties in the Transgeled, worked her way up to Commander, and received a Distinguished Service Medal for action against pirates near Cothar. From TE 152 to TE 154 she was assigned to the Tep Kecor squadron and there came under the inspiring influence of her commander, Rear Admiral Chev Fonnel. With Fonnel's assistance, Thovold was selected to attend the Navy's command and general staff school at Hafen. Then a Commodore, she graduated first in a class of 2200 in TE 146, and two years later she graduated from the Navy War College. She then served in Credix, writing a textbook on Formation Wars strategy and tactics, and in Patala before becoming an aide to Terran Fleet Admiral Donatela Padgham in 163.

Two years later she accompanied Padgham to Credix to assist in the reorganization of Naval operations, and there was awarded the rank of Rear Admiral and put in command of the Deletia Wing. She soon won the attention of Supreme Admiral Toris Gund for her role in planning war games involving the entire Credix and Phuctra fleets.

In 171, Gund appointed Thovold head of the operations division of the Imperial Navy on Terra. In June 172, Gund selected her over 120 senior officers to replace the retiring Padgham as Terran Fleet

Admiral. When Gund retired in 175, the Imperial Council accepted his recommendation and promoted Thovold to Supreme Admiral.

Thovold's advancement in the Navy was due not only to her knowledge of military strategy and a talent for organization, but also to her ability to persuade, to mediate, and to be agreeable. Men and women from a variety of backgrounds and planets, impressed by her friendliness, humility, and persistent optimism, liked and trusted her.

In 179, when Geled's seat on the Imperial Council went vacant, Planetary Governor Delia Tattersall appointed Thovold to the seat. The following year, she won re-election handily.

In the next five years, Thovold's reputation in the Imperial Council grew as she built up alliances and avoided scandal, proving herself to be both a loyal friend and a tower of personal and professional integrity. As early as 180 she was mentioned as a candidate for Secretary-General. Her personal qualities and military reputation prompted all parties to woo her. As the campaign of 184 neared, Thovold let it be known that her sympathies lay with the Unionist Party, which advocated closer ties between the Provinces and more central control by the Empire. The Party's head, Trev Fodon, made an intensive effort to persuade her to seek the office.

Thovold campaigned tirelessly, impressing the population with her warmth and sincerity. She urged closer co-operation between Provinces, honesty in government, and promised to visit each Province to explore options for tighter unification of the Empire as a whole. At the same time, Unionists spoke of corruption among the ruling Leonov-Lütken coalition, and attacked the administration of Secretary-General Vernon Castiligoni for graft and influence peddling. Thovold forged an alliance with the Carroll-LaVerne-Fodon opposition, and together with the Unionists they won a majority in the Council elections of 184, and Thovold was confirmed as Secretary-General.

Because of her military background and limited knowledge of government, Thovold delegated authority to her advisers and Cabinet members and did not participate actively in the detailed work of administration. Her assistant, Tovi Baravic, was a powerful figure in the administration. Thovold expected her staff to boil down, simplify, and expedite the urgent business that had to be brought to her attention, and to keep as much work of secondary importance as possible off her desk.

Through her secretaries of commerce and technology, Thovold decreased Imperial control over the economy and encouraged economic activity across Provincial borders, something which had been discouraged by the Leonov-Lütken coalition. She also used the Navy as a tool of integration, encouraging task forces composed of ships and personnel from different Fleets. In 186 the Navy put down a rebellion in Credix, and Thovold appeared personally to command the successful co-ordinated effort.

Thovold played Idara against Idara, while at the same time building support among the mercantile sector. By 187, she had developed an unassailable coalition in the Council, and commanded the absolute loyalty of the Imperial Navy. On Empire Day 187, with the Imperial Council in recess, Maj Thovold placed Navy garrisons around the homeworlds of the major opposition Idara, then appeared on a galaxy-wide broadcast to address the Empire. Her stirring speech, which lasted a bare fifteen minutes, dwelt on the dangers of fractionalism and the benefits of unity, and she finished:

> "If we continue along our current path, our great Empire will splinter into eight or more little Empires. We will become hounds squabbling over our meat; jackals, fighting over a pitiful corpse.

> "My fellow citizens, I do not believe that this is the destiny we want. I do not believe—*will* not believe—that you have put me here to preside over the dissolution of this Empire which our ancestors struggled and fought to create. Just as we are one people, all sharing the common blood of Terra—so I say that we are one culture, one race, one Empire. And I swear to you, I will not allow this Empire to splinter. I will not allow the forces of greed and vanity to tear us apart. I will do everything within my power to preserve this Union. With your help, I shall establish a new peace, a Pax Terranica that will last far beyond our time.

> "When Joradankov and the Founders created this Empire, they gave us a Throne and a Crown, as symbols of our essential unity. And to protect us from despotism, they chose to leave that Throne vacant, that Crown unlifted. Today I come before you, in this time of crisis, to ask your permission to lift that Crown, to take that Throne. I ask your permission to establish, once and for all, one rule that will unite the sons and daughters of Terra. Humbled in the sight of the Heavens and before the souls of our ancestors, I ask that you make your will known, to the Council and to your other officials. Shall we continue on our current path of

destruction, or shall we lift the torch of liberty, and take the path that will lead to a new peace?"

Public response was tremendous, and Thovold's display of military power was most convincing. The opposition could do nothing but refuse to vote. By a vote of 161 to 2 (with 38 abstentions), the Council sent Thovold a formal request that she take the Throne as the Terran Empire's first Empress. The position of Secretary-General was eliminated entirely. On Solstice Day TE 187, Maj Thovold was formally crowned.

Thovold's reign was a peaceful and successful time for the Empire. The economy boomed, as the number of inhabited planets nearly doubled. She worked tirelessly to curb the power of the Idara and to integrate the separate parts of the Empire. A wholesale reorganization of the Civil Service (190-196) was quite successful in breaking down regionalism and separatist feelings.

The most notable event of Maj Thovold's reign was the Engelbach Rebellion of 196-7. Dissidents, co-ordinated by the Idara Engelbach of Leikeis, held a galaxy-wide labor strike in protest against Thovold's rule. On the eleventh day of the strike, approximately 30,000 leaders were arrested and exiled to the Tarantula Nebula. Historians view the Engelbach Rebellion as demonstration that Thovold's power was still largely dependent on the Imperial Navy. However, it set the precedent that the Throne was more powerful than the nobility. The Imperial Council learned quickly…and resented.

The Tarantula dissidents proved to be her ultimate undoing. In 219, during a military expedition to the Tarantula Nebula, Thovold met her death in combat with rebels. Her hand-picked successor, Tsung-Dao Wu, became Emperor upon her death.

From *Encyclopedia Terranica*, New York, Terra, TE 375:

Wu, Tsung-Dao

Emperor of the Terran Empire TE 219-235

b. 16 September TE 167 Odonia
d. 19 March TE 235 New York, Terra

Tsung-Dao Wu, son of Tsung-Kun Wu and Mowra Cinq-Mars, was born nearly three months after his father's death. His father was Planetary Governor of Odonia, and his mother was a former delegate to the Imperial Council and regional supervisor for Rockwell Interstellar. When the boy was six, his mother was promoted to Operations Co-ordinator for Sol Province, and the family moved to Terra. In New York, London, and Beijing, Tsung-Dao was raised in an atmosphere of corporate and Idara intrigue. By the time he passed his adulthood exams at 16, the young man was quite at home with the Terran political scene.

In TE 185, at age 18, he was appointed to the Imperial Council as representative of Rockwell. In the Council, Tsung-Dao was one of a group of young populists known in the press as the Knights of the Round Table.

In TE 189, at age 22, Tsung-Dao was apprehended on Kybos and tried for fomenting rebellion against Imperial rule. He was deported to the Tarantula Nebula. While in Tarantula, he founded several enclaves for mutual co-operation. He ruled for a time (TE 194-196) over a "state" of about 10^5 cubic kilometers, until he was thrown out in a dispute over breeding policies.

About TE 201 Tsung-Dao was contacted by Brin Lütken and Catherine Leonov, and he began running tachyon vesicle pickups to an uninhabited system near Deletia. He was put in charge of logistics for Tarantula Fleet construction in TE 208, and appointed Internal Security Minister of the Tarantula Rebel State in TE 212.

About this time, Tsung-Dao began to have a change of heart about Brin and Catherine and tried to establish ways to get around them. He developed schemes to remove them if and when when the Empress was overthrown.

In TE 219, he was closely involved in the Tarantula Incident in which Maj Thovold defeated Brin and Catherine. Tsung-Dao was rather surprised to find himself named as Thovold's chosen successor.

In TE 219, when Tsung-Dao Wu was fighting to consolidate his Imperial power, he gained support among Idara Lütken and Idara Kasmanski by gifting Lütken with the Duchies of Credix and Geled, and Kasmanski with Borshall. Of course, he also angered Chen, Cepeda and Carcopino—but this move was calculated to cut down the influence of Chen, which had grown very powerful in charge of Credix.

In 225, Tsung-Dao became aware of Ami Kuchta, a 16-year-old scion of Idara Kuchta who was starting a quick rise through the Imperial bureaucracy. He took an immediate liking to the girl, seeing in her a reflection of his own early self. Soon, Ami Kuchta became the daughter Tsung-Dao had never had, and in 231 he formally adopted her, naming her as his chosen successor.

Tsung-Dao Wu died on Terra in TE 235, at the age of 67, and was succeeded by Ami Kuchta.

Timeline

2153 CE /TE 0 - Terran Empire founded

TE 37 - Provincial Capitals established

TE 120 - Terran Empire effectively controls all Human-settled planets of the Galaxy]

TE 123 - Maj Thovold born

TE 167 - Tsung-Dao Wu born

TE 184 - Maj Thovold elected Secretary-General

TE 187 - Maj Thovold crowned Empress

TE 189 - Tsung-Dao Wu deported to Tarantula

TE 192 - Paula Adelhardt born

TE 197 - Engelbach Rebellion

TE 219 - Tarantula Incident

Scattered Worlds Chronological Sequence

0.0 (before 2.4 billion BCE) - PRE-PYLISTROPH; Sapient life in the Gathered Worlds

1.0 (c. 2.4 billion BCE) - THE PYLISTROPH; Seed Vessels launched

2.0 (c. 1.2 billion BCE) - GERGATHAN PROCLAIMS MERTORTHAR
Flight of the Daamin; Schism of the Hlutr; Empires of the Scattered Worlds

3.0 (c. 100,000 BCE) - PRE-IMPERIAL TERRA
3.75 (2042 CE) - *Dance for the Ivory Madonna*
3.85 (20698 CE) - *Hunt for the Dymalon Cygnet*
3.962 (2103 CE) - "Gamester"
3.968 (2103 CE) - "Big Improvement"

4.0 (2153 CE/TE 0) - FIRST TERRAN EMPIRE
4.55 (TE 219) - *Weaving the Web of Days*
4.74 (TE 321) - *The Eighth Succession*
4.75 (TE 335) - *Children of the Eighth Day*
4.852 (TE k361) - "Candelabra and Diamonds"
4.882 (TE 403) - *A Voice in Every Wind*

5.0 (2624 CE) - INTERREGNUM
5.38 (6484 CE) - *A Rose From Old Terra*

6.0 (2488 CE/12,488 HE) - FEDERATION OF FAMILIES
6.55 (c. 17,700 HE) "The Geas Ingenerate"

7.0 (20,724 HE) - SECOND TERRAN EMPIRE

8.0 (24,356 HE) - POST-IMPERIAL HUMANITY
8.5 (c. 30,000 HE) - *The Leaves of October*

9.0 (c. 3 million HE) - ENDTIME

The Scattered Worlds Mosaic by Don Sakers

Dance for the Ivory Madonna
a romance of psiberspace
Print & Kindle

Spectrum Award finalist; 56 Hugo nominations
*"Imagine a Stand on Zanzibar written by a left-wing Robert Heinlein, and infused with the most exciting possibilities of the new cyber-technology." -Melissa Scott,
author of Dreaming Metal, The Jazz*

Weaving the Web of Days
a tale of the Scattered Worlds
Print & Kindle

Maj Thovold has led the Galaxy for three decades, a Golden Age of peace and prosperity. She is weary and ready to resign, but she faces one last battle: a battle on the strangest battlefield known: a web of living tendrils that stretches across interstellar space. A web where Maj's enemies wait, like spiders, for their prey....

The Eighth Succession
a novel of the Scattered Worlds
Print & Kindle

"Remember when science fiction used to be filled with galactic intrigue and bigger-than-life heroes? The wonderful Don Sakers certainly does! The Eighth Succession is a rip-roaring yarn, impossible to put down. If John W. Campbell's Astounding Stories had been published in an LGBT-friendly era, this is the cover-story serial you'd have been waiting anxiously for each month. What a ride!" -Robert J. Sawyer, Hugo Award-winning author of Red Planet Blues

Children of the Eighth Day
a novel of the Scattered Worlds
Print & Kindle

The Eighth Succession *introduced readers to the Hoister Family...*
Children of the Eighth Day *takes the story of this remarkable family to the exciting next level.*

The Scattered Worlds Mosaic by Don Sakers

All Roads Lead to Terra
two tales of the Scattered Worlds
Kindle only
Two exciting tales tell of attacks against the shining jewel of the Terran Empire: Earth. Includes an introduction and notes from the author.

A Voice in Every Wind
two tales of the Scattered Worlds
Print & Kindle
On a world where meaning lives in every rock and stream, and every breeze brings a new voice, one human explorer stands on the threshold of discoveries that could alter the future of Humanity.

A Rose From Old Terra
a novel of the Scattered Worlds
Print & Kindle
Jedrek left the Grand Library and his work circle eleven years ago. Now a crisis in uncharted space brings the circle back together. Soon, Jedrek and his friends are at the focal point of a clash of cultures, and the only thing that can save the Galaxy is one modest group of Librarians.

The Leaves of October
a novel of the Scattered Worlds
Print & Kindle
Compton Crook Award finalist
The Hlutr: Immensely old, terribly wise…and utterly alien. When mankind went out into the stars, he found the Hlutr waiting for him. Waiting to observe, to converse, to help. Waiting to judge…and, if necessary, to destroy.

More Books from Speed-of-C Productions

The Curse of the Zwilling by Don Sakers
Print & Kindle
It's Hogwarts meets Buffy at Patapsco University: a small, cozy liberal arts college like so many others – except for the Department of Comparative Religion, where age-old spells are taught and magic is practiced. When a favorite teacher is found dead under mysterious circumstances, grad student David Galvin finds that a malevolent evil has awakened. And now David, along with four novice undergrads, must defeat this ancient, malignant terror.

The SF Book of Days by Don Sakers
Print only
Drawn from the pages of classic sf literature, here is a science fiction/fantasy event for every day of the year…and for quite a few days that aren't part of the year. From Doc Brown's arrival in Hill Valley (January 1, 1885) to the launch of the Bellerophon *(Sextor 7, 2351), this datebook is truly out of this world.*

PsiScouts #1: At Risk by Don Sakers & Phil Meade
Print & Kindle
In the 26th century, psi-powered teenagers from all over the Myriad Worlds join together as the heroic PsiScouts.

PsiScouts #2: Bright Promise by Don Sakers & Phil Meade
Print & Kindle
Further adventures of the heroic PsiScouts in the 26th century.

Meat and Machine: queer writings by Don Sakers
Print & Kindle
Don Sakers has been queering sf and fantasy for three decades. Meat and Machine collects 24 short pieces of Don's science fiction, fantasy, nonfiction, and erotics.

Elevenses by Don Sakers
Print & Kindle
Eleven SF and fantasy short stories intended as bite-size snacks.

More Books from Speed-of-C Productions

Gaylaxicon Sampler 2006
Print only
Sample the work of thirteen writers from across the spectrum of gay, lesbian, bisexual, and/or transgender science fiction, fantasy, and/or horror. Includes big names and small, much-published veterans and promising beginners, Lammy and Spectrum Award nominees and winners, past Gaylaxicon Guests of Honor, and fresh new names.

QSpec Sampler 2007
Print only
Originally prepared as a giveaway at Gaylaxicon 2007 in Atlanta, this volume is available at a nominal charge as a sampler of the fine work being done by GLBT writers in SF, fantasy, and horror.

Lucky in Love by Don Sakers
Print & Kindle
When his best friend Keith moved away, there was a big hole left in Frank's life. Then a bad car crash put him in the hospital. While there recovering, he got a visit from the star of his high school basketball team, Purnell Johnson. It wasn't long before his luck started to improve.

Five Planes by Melissa Scott & Don Sakers
Print & Kindle
Space opera adventure. Pirates. Judges. Weird physics. Desperate refugees. Struggling colonists. Missing persons and a mystery ship. A quest for human origins in a pocket universe.

A Cosmos of Many Mansions: Varieties of SF by Don Sakers
Print & Kindle
Based on the first five years of Sakers's popular review column, this volume examines & explains dozens of types of science fiction along with hundreds of reviews.

The Mud of the Place by Susanna J. Sturgis
Print only
"A sensitive, witty, and tightly plotted portrayal of life on Martha's Vineyard that only a true Islander could have written. Nice going, Susanna!" –Cynthia Riggs